Praise for Claire Thompson's
Polar Reaction

Rating: 5 Hearts "...You just have to love it when three men are stranded in Antarctica together! Just the story's concept will draw you in, then the love story begins and you are hooked. Claire Thompson proves herself with this unconventional romance. ...Polar Reaction is a must read for anyone who loves gay romance."

~ *April, The Romance Studio*

Rating: 4 Angels "...Polar Reaction is a touching and erotic story of three men, learning about themselves and each other. I enjoyed learning the deepest emotional parts of each man and was touched by their love and struggles. Claire Thompson is a master at creating in-depth characters and perfectly illustrating who they are and how they feel."

~ *Melissa, Fallen Angel Reviews*

"...The sexual chemistry between Brendan, Tuck and Jamie is delicious and explosive. The plot is entertaining. I really felt the fear and stress of the being stranded along with the heroes. ...I was constantly on edge wondering if they would be rescued and what would happen..."

~ *Christina, Romance Junkies*

"Claire Thompson's Polar Reaction is a story about the complexities of a ménage relationship and one man's struggle to come to terms with his sexual identity. This story is well written with an interesting plot, complex characters, and a narrative that flows with an almost effortless style...This is a very sensual novel that concentrates on an unusual kind of relationship – a ménage a trois...If you want to step just a little outside of the usual box, you may wish to give Polar Reaction a shot."

~ *BD Whitney, Bookwenches.com*

"Polar Reaction is an emotionally stimulating love story...Claire Thompson has created a superb, well written tale that illustrates three men equal in a devoted and compassionate relationship. Polar Reaction is an impressive saga that I enjoyed immensely."

~ *Chocolate Minx, Literary Nymphs Reviews*

"Take three guys who are secretly attracted to each other and strand them together indefinitely and you get a few very hot nights. Tender feelings and intense desire create a tumultuous and angst-filled relationship...The dynamics between the men are fun and intense. Brendan's hesitancy, and excitement, is endearing, Jamie's experience and submissiveness is hot, and Tuck's assertiveness is sexy. Polar Reaction is not just an erotic romance, it's a good story too."

~ *Nikki, Rainbow Reviews*

Look for these titles by
Claire Thompson

Now Available:

Handyman
Our Man Friday

Polar Reaction

Claire Thompson

A Samhain Publishing, Ltd. publication.

Samhain Publishing, Ltd.
577 Mulberry Street, Suite 1520
Macon, GA 31201
www.samhainpublishing.com

Polar Reaction
Copyright © 2010 by Claire Thompson
Print ISBN: 978-1-60504-455-2
Digital ISBN: 978-1-60504-462-0

Editing by Sasha Knight
Cover by Anne Cain

First Samhain Publishing, Ltd. electronic publication: March 2009
First Samhain Publishing, Ltd. print publication: January 2010

Chapter One

Brendan stood like the perfect wet dream beneath the spray, his erect cock clutched in his hand. The shower curtain was open only a few inches, but it was enough to see the handsome man, head slumped against his chest with eyes closed, fingers flying. Tuck knew he should make some noise, let Brendan know he was in the bathroom, but he couldn't move.

Instead Tuck stood frozen, hungrily watching the man he'd dreamed of possessing ever since he'd first laid eyes on him the year before. They'd worked together on the Blue Glacier Project in Washington's Olympic Mountains. Though Brendan billed himself as straight, Tuck had his doubts, especially after that night around the campfire. They had stayed up long after the rest of the crew had straggled off to bed, talking about their dreams and hopes.

The connection had been immediate and, for Tuck at least, intense. It wasn't their shared passion for the research they did, or Brendan's wide, easy smile. It wasn't the sexy curve of his muscular thigh beneath faded blue denim. It wasn't the way the firelight had flickered on his cheek, lighting the thick fall of curling blond hair down his strong neck and reflecting the heat of desire Tuck felt for him. Or rather, it was all of those things and more. It was the *more*—that indefinable attraction that once in a blue moon grabbed you by the throat and wouldn't let go, no matter how hard you tried to forget or deny...

That night by the fire, though admittedly aided by several bottles of beer, Tuck had felt the crackle of desire arc between them like heat lightning. He had experimented, leaning close until their thighs touched. Where a straight guy would have shifted and pulled away, Brendan had remained still. If anything, he had moved closer.

They had shared stories of their lives, both funny and sad, lowering their defenses in a way that was rare between men. When Tuck dared to put a comforting arm around Brendan's shoulders, he hadn't pulled away. If it had been up to Tuck, they would have remained thigh to thigh, heads nearly touching until the sun came up.

It hadn't gone any further, but Tuck had seen the bulge beneath Brendan's jeans which matched his own. He had seen, for a lingering moment, the longing mirrored in Brendan's eyes.

Now on their last day in the Antarctic, there Brendan stood like a Greek god, the head of his thick, long cock emerging from his curled fingers like a promise, his eyes squeezed tight as he neared his goal.

If you were mine... Tuck mouthed.

If he were Tuck's lover, Brendan wouldn't need to masturbate. Tuck would wake him each morning by scooting down beneath the sheets, his mouth and hands seeking Brendan's warm, naked body. He wouldn't touch the shaft—not right away. First he would lick Brendan's balls, gliding over the soft, loose flesh, inhaling the rich musk of his lover.

He would take each ball into his mouth, worshipping it with his tongue, his lips, the slightest nudge of his teeth. Brendan would stir in his sleep but not fully waken. Tuck would push his lover's thighs apart and lower his head. With a feather-light touch, he would tongue the tiny puckered entrance, which later he would plunder while Brendan knelt on his hands and knees, spreading himself for Tuck's tender but insistent invasion.

When Brendan's cock was engorged, Tuck would grab the base of it and lower his mouth over its satin heat. He would take his time, licking, sucking, bringing him nearly to the edge, only to pull back to watch the play of raw emotion slide over Brendan's face.

He wouldn't let Brendan come until he begged for it. Then he would apply himself with the dedication of a desperate man, taking the length of Brendan's shaft deep into his throat, not letting go until he'd siphoned every precious drop.

Tuck pressed his palm hard against his erection through the denim, his mind filled with the fantasy, his eyes filled with the vision of the gorgeous, naked man before him. What would happen if he stripped off his clothes and entered the shower stall, kneeling in front of Brendan, pushing his hands away so he could take the shaft lovingly between his lips?

He would cup Brendan's balls while sucking him to ecstasy. Would Brendan keep his eyes squeezed shut and pretend it was a woman at his feet? Or would he open them and whisper Tuck's name with grateful wonder?

Who was he kidding? Brendan would probably yell for Tuck to get the hell away, if he didn't punch him in the jaw first.

Brendan half-turned as he began to ejaculate, drawing Tuck's eye to his muscular, small ass in profile. Tuck's balls ached, his cock twisting uncomfortably in his jeans. In a moment Brendan would open his eyes. He would see Tuck there, spying on him, the raw lust naked in his eyes. Wrenching himself from the sexy scene, Tuck slipped away.

"Gin." Jamie Hunter slapped the cards down on the table with a flourish and grinned. It was the last night before the final plane returned to carry him, along with David Tucker and Brendan Aaronson, back to civilization. The rest of the twenty-one-man lab crew had been airlifted out the day before, as February moved to a close, signaling the onset of winter in the Southern Hemisphere.

At the last minute they'd decided to take back some equipment for calibration, so there ended up being a shortage of space on the plane sent to collect the crew. The three scientists had volunteered to stay the extra two nights until a plane could return for them.

Jamie, at twenty-five the youngest guy on the team, had been thrilled to get the position as research assistant. He owed the assignment to Tuck, who worked with him at the Wexler Institute in Monterey. Dr. Tucker, who worked in a different lab and, Jamie had thought, barely knew he existed, had recommended Jamie for the position when someone had dropped out at the last minute.

It was an incredible project to be involved in, with recent advances in deep core drilling technology enabling their drilling engineers to extrude core samples from the ice divide that contained an accumulation of snow and ice from previous time periods. The composition of these ice cores would allow them to study greenhouse gas emissions over forty thousand years.

Tuck and Brendan, both with PhDs in molecular bioscience and some major publications already under their belts, were regarded as experts in the field. Jamie admired them both for their work and dedication, but he couldn't deny he also admired them for their seriously hot looks.

Tuck was the tall, dark and handsome one, with straight black hair, deep-set dark eyes and a sexy five-o'clock shadow even when he'd just shaved. Jamie had been aware of him back at the labs in California, but had never had the chance to get to know him. He'd seen him from time to time in the company of women and had just assumed he was straight. Beyond that, he'd always promised himself never to get involved with someone he worked with and so far that policy had stead him well.

Brendan, with gray green eyes and a muscular build, had sun-streaked blond hair curling down the back of his neck and a spectacular smile that made Jamie's heart clutch the rare times it had been bestowed upon him.

The only available place to jerk off was in the shower stall, since the men shared sleeping quarters. Many hot scenarios involving both Tuck and Brendan, together and alone, had played through Jamie's mind while he pumped himself to a rapid orgasm, mindful not to use up the hot water before the next guy had his turn.

Not that he'd ever given either guy the slightest indication of his attraction to them over the six weeks they'd been in such close quarters. Though he never pretended to be straight, nor did Jamie advertise his homosexuality. It was nobody's business. Especially not in the confines of an enclosed science lab built on a slab of ice in the middle of nowhere, with no way out if things became awkward. Nevertheless, a guy could dream.

Tuck threw down his hands with mock exasperation. "What, again? Are you sure these cards aren't marked?"

"Food's ready." Brendan leaned his head into the sleeping quarters where Tuck and Jamie were playing cards. All the cots had been stripped of their bedding, except for their three, still covered with sheets and bright red thick down quilts.

The kitchen was located just off the sleeping quarters and tonight Brendan had volunteered to make the meal. As they sat at the long table, now set only for three, Jamie glanced out the window. "Hey, it's snowing." The other two men looked up.

"I noticed a storm system working its way toward us on the radar." Brendan frowned. "I didn't think it'd get here so quick, though. It wasn't predicted to get this far until sometime after we flew out in the morning. Hopefully it won't affect our plans." They watched the whirling snow for several moments. It was falling fast, though the winds seemed relatively calm.

"Well, nothing we can do about it now," Brendan continued philosophically. "In the morning we can shovel out and make sure there's a decent landing strip for the plane. Meanwhile, help yourselves to my specialty."

They dug into the plates of spaghetti and meatballs he had set before them, which was the only thing Jamie had seen Brendan make when it was his turn to cook. He'd made lemonade from a powdered mix to go with it. Though there was still some canned and packaged food in the pantries, food that would be left in the lab over the winter, the refrigerated supplies had been depleted in anticipation of the project's end.

The whole place had been cleared out, all the expensive lab equipment carefully packed and removed to labs in warmer climes until the work resumed in October. Without all the usual hubbub of the rest of the crew, the place was empty, almost lonely.

"Hey, I almost forgot. I was saving this for a special occasion. Be right back." In a moment Tuck returned, waving a bottle of wine toward them. He pulled a Swiss army knife from his pocket and used the small corkscrew to remove the cork.

The lab not being equipped with wineglasses, Brendan

retrieved three juice glasses from the cabinet. Jamie watched as Tuck filled them. He noticed, not for the first time, Tuck's large hands and long, thick fingers and marveled how he could handle delicate scientific equipment with the precision and accuracy that he did. He couldn't help the road along which his thoughts invariably meandered, wondering how his hand size compared to other parts of his anatomy...

Tuck lifted his glass in a toast, jerking Jamie from his sexual speculation. "To a job well done. I can't believe it's ending already. You guys have been really great to work with." He turned to Jamie with a smile. "Jamie, your support over these weeks has been invaluable. You should have more than enough data to complete your dissertation, but beyond that, you're making a vital contribution to the global scientific community."

"Thanks." Jamie felt curiously let down by the rather formal commendation, though he appreciated it. He stared at Tuck, searching for something more personal behind the words.

If he hadn't been scrutinizing him so closely, he might have missed the sudden glimpse of desperate yearning that flashed over his features as Tuck turned to Brendan. As quickly as it had appeared, it was gone, Tuck's face again composed into a bland smile as he offered praise for Brendan as innocuous as that which he'd offered Jamie.

The meal over, they washed and put away the dishes. "It's weird having nothing to do, with the labs emptied out," Tuck observed, as they settled on the beat-up old sofa in their sleeping quarters to watch a video on Brendan's large laptop.

Brendan assumed his team leader persona. "We could do some more analysis on the latest ice core readings. I have some detailed graphs worked up—"

Both Jamie and Tucker threw their pillows at him. He lifted

his hands in surrender, laughing. "Okay, okay. We'll watch a movie."

The room was dark, save for the silvered light emanating from the screen, etching the profiles of Brendan and Jamie beside him. Both appeared to be engrossed in the film but Tuck couldn't have even said what it was about. All he could think of was Brendan, who sat so close he could reach over and touch his thigh.

It was hard to believe this was their last night together. Tuck and Jamie would return to their lab in Monterey—Brendan to his research at the Kramer Institute in Washington State. Was he really going to blow it again? To let Brendan get away without even telling him how he felt?

He'd hoped to find a way during this project to get closer to Brendan—to try to rekindle the heat he now wondered if maybe he'd only imagined because his own desire loomed so large. Yet in the six weeks they'd been working on the Antarctica project, he'd had no opportunity to be alone with Brendan.

They had played several games of football on calm afternoons with some of the other guys. Though the air was below freezing it felt much warmer with the sun reflecting off the white snow causing them to sweat beneath their layers.

Each time they'd been on opposite teams and each time Tuck had managed to tackle Brendan, the only physical contact he dared to make.

Two days before, Brendan had been the one to bring Tuck down onto the hard-packed snow. He'd fallen heavily over Tuck as they grappled for the ball. When he'd landed, they'd been cheek to cheek for a moment, Brendan's breath crystallizing in the air just beside Tuck's ear. He'd had a nearly uncontrollable desire to pull Brendan's face to his and kiss him.

Brendan had lain on top of him for several long, tantalizing seconds, during which Tuck's cock had risen hard against Brendan's thigh. Brendan scrambled up, catching Tuck's gaze. Tuck could have sworn he'd seen something there—a spark of desire—secret and fleeting, but undeniable.

Back when they'd worked together the prior year, Brendan had just broken up with a girlfriend he'd been seeing for a while. Tuck still remembered the conversation, especially Brendan's seemingly offhand comment: "I just don't get women, you know? Sometimes I think it would be easier to be involved with a guy. At least they say what they mean. You know where you stand."

"Yeah, I know what you mean," Tuck had agreed, not daring back then to follow up in a more serious vein. As he thought over the conversation several hundred times over the next year, he had to laugh at the irony of Brendan's remark. Tuck certainly hadn't said what he meant and as far as he knew, Brendan had no clue Tuck was attracted to him.

They'd lost touch and though Tuck had thought many times about him, he hadn't taken any real action to find him. He couldn't stand to take the chance of a rebuff, which was almost surely what would happen if he made his feelings known.

Tuck, who hated to fail, no matter what the endeavor, tried to tell himself it was just a passing infatuation, based on as little as the moss green of Brendan's eyes, which crinkled into half moons when he smiled.

Yet how Tuck's heart had leapt when he had been offered a position as a research analyst on the West Antarctic Deep Ice

Project, and discovered Brendan Aaronson was on the roster. He'd decided then it was fate that they meet again and this time, he'd vowed, he would find a way to let Brendan know his feelings, and then let the chips fall where they may.

But the six weeks had come and gone, each of them extremely busy with their work. With the communal, cramped sleeping quarters and twenty-one guys always milling around, there had been little-to-no opportunity to make his feelings known.

Maybe it wasn't too late. Maybe on the plane ride back to the States he would make a move.

It took Brendan a moment to realize he was awake. The low, whistling howl that had manifested itself as wolves in his dream was in fact a tearing wind. The frame of their modular building shuddered, causing a ripple in the insulated fabric covering the walls and ceiling.

Brendan sat up, reaching for the flashlight beneath his cot. He clicked it on and shone it around the room. Both the other men were sleeping, Jamie completely hidden beneath his quilt, Tuck with one arm flung over his face.

Brendan stood and walked over to the window. He pulled back the insulated flap. It was pitch black outside, the wind louder without the muffle of fabric, the glass rattling and icy to the touch. He looked at his watch. It was still a few hours until sunrise. Taking his laptop with him so he wouldn't disturb the others, he made his way through the kitchen and down the narrow hallway toward the wet lab.

Flicking on the light, he sat at the workstation and booted

up his computer. When he opened the browser to check the weather, he found there was no Internet connection. The site was set up to receive satellite cell and Internet service and in the time they'd been there, it had worked fine. They'd experienced some weather-degraded performance during high winds before, but it usually reinitialized within a few minutes.

He shut down the computer and gave it a cold boot, but when he tried again there was still no connection. Returning to the sleeping quarters, he fished in his pants pocket for his cell phone and flipped it open. There was no service.

Brendan slipped back under the covers and stowed the flashlight beneath his cot. Closing his eyes, he told himself not to worry. Probably the storm would pass by morning. A few hours delay wouldn't make much difference in the scheme of things.

He was awakened by someone shaking his shoulder. "Brendan, wake up." Jamie's voice was urgent and tinged with panic. "I got up to bulldoze the landing strip but I can't even open the door. It's blocked by snow drifts."

Brendan sat up, instantly awake. Tuck came out of the bathroom, wiping his face with a towel. Brendan turned toward him. "Jamie says we're snowed in. When I woke last night, I tried to get the Internet to check the forecasts but we had no access." He reached for his cell phone again, flipping it open. No service.

"It's still snowing, from what I can see out the windows." Jamie peered out. "And the wind is insane. Listen to it." The building was shuddering and creaking from the gale-force winds, which whistled and howled like the wolves in Brendan's dream.

Tuck sat heavily on his cot. "We're not going anywhere in this weather, that's for sure. The wind is whipping up the snow already on the surface. No way a plane could land in these blinding conditions. If you were out there, you wouldn't even be able to see a few feet in front of you, much less find a landing strip."

"We're not going to get any satellite transmissions either," Brendan observed. "The maximum operating wind speed for the satellite dish is sixty miles per hour. From the sound of it, those winds are gusting at over a hundred."

"Oh my God, you mean we're *stranded*?" Jamie's voice rose.

Brendan could hear the edge of hysteria in Jamie's tone. "Hey, take it easy. We've got enough provisions to last a month here if we had to. We have our portable oil-burning heaters and the propane stove in the kitchen. The diesel generators have enough fuel to power the whole building for at least a week. If we shut down the labs and only heat this immediate area, we could keep it comfortably habitable for a month."

"In a month it'll be deep winter." Jamie bit his lip.

"Relax, this thing is going to pass in a day or two." Brendan put his hand on the younger man's shoulder and, forcing down his own trepidation, smiled. "We'll be fine. I promise."

Chapter Two

"How can he concentrate with this damn wind?" Slanted white sheets of snow continued to hurl against all sides of the building and the sun had forgotten to rise. Jamie refused to entertain the frightening scenario trying to press its way into his brain—the building being blown apart like a toy house made of matchsticks, the three of them buried alive in the icy freeze, each helpless to save the others or himself as nature inexorably reclaimed them in death. He shook his head, trying to dislodge the images. He was overreacting. Brendan was right—this would be over in a few hours. By tomorrow they would be rescued.

Jamie peered through the open door that led from the sleeping quarters into the kitchen. Brendan was sitting at the table, a mug of coffee beside his open laptop, his fingers moving steadily over the keys.

Tuck looked up from his novel at Jamie's question. "Brendan Aaronson could concentrate in an avalanche. It's one of the reason's he's so productive. He can analyze a hundred pages of data in the time it would take most people to sift through twenty. He focuses like a laser beam. He won't even hear you talking directly to him when he's concentrating like that."

Jamie nodded, thinking of his own work—the pages and

pages of notes and raw data heaped in his laptop like a pile of straw he hoped eventually to weave into gold. Maybe he would work on the outline—distract himself as Brendan seemed to be doing so successfully. He could put on headphones and blast his music, drowning out that menacing, howling wind.

Jamie looked at Tuck, stretched out on his cot, the very pose of relaxed ease. Tuck was tall, taller than Jamie's six feet, his legs long and muscular, his shoulders broad. Not for the first time, Jamie imagined what it would be like to slide his own bare body against Tuck's, to feel the rise of Tuck's cock against him as their lips parted for a kiss.

He'd been honored when Tuck had suggested him to fill the assistant research spot, but had to force himself not to assign more meaning to it than there was. The pace was so intense and involved during the course of their research, he hadn't had a chance to explore any possible interest on Tuck's side. Maybe once they were rescued he'd consider breaking his own rule about no involvement with colleagues and test the waters.

If they got rescued.

Stop it. Jamie shut his eyes and rolled his head in an effort to relax the knotted tendons in his neck.

Tuck closed his book, stood and walked to the couch. Sitting, he patted the spot beside him. "Hey, why don't you sit down, Jamie? You're pacing the room like a caged lion. It's going to be okay. Really. We just need to be patient. This structure was designed to withstand these kinds of storms and there are more than enough provisions. We're warm and safe."

Jamie sat, facing Tuck. "You're right, I know." He shook his head. "I keep thinking about the weather back home. About my little cottage by the sea. I can't wait to get back."

"Yeah. But think of the great story we'll have to tell, right? It'll be headline news." Tuck waved his hand in the air, as if reading a huge banner hanging there. "Three Scientists Rescued From the Edge of the World." He turned a devilish smile on Jamie. "And think of the fun we can have while we're waiting. Why, there's no end of mischief we could get up to."

Jamie's gut flip-flopped, his cock perking to attention. Was it his imagination, or was Tuck making an offer? What about the women he'd seen Tuck with back in California? But then, he'd seen him with guys too. Maybe he went both ways.

He recalled the way Tuck had looked at Brendan the night before, the longing palpable in his face. Yeah, there was a pretty good chance Tuck was at least curious, but how far did it go? Did he know Jamie was gay?

It was tempting to find out, but did he dare? They still had to work together back in the States. What if Jamie's hunch was wrong? Maybe he could work it so any overture on his part could be couched in other terms. Like the old aching-muscles gambit. Which in his case wouldn't even be a lie. He was so tense from the storm, his neck felt like twisted iron. Deciding to go for it, he gripped the back of his neck and winced for Tuck's benefit.

"You okay?" Tuck asked.

"Me? Yeah. Tense, I guess. Or maybe I slept funny. My neck's killing me."

Tuck smiled, white teeth against olive skin. "You're in luck. I'm known for my killer massage technique."

Jamie suppressed a smile. So far so good. He crossed his legs to hide the instant erection the offer of a massage had produced. He made sure his voice remained casual. "Okay. I mean, if you don't mind."

"Not at all. Take off the flannel shirt, why don't you. It's plenty warm in here. Then I can get at you better." Tuck arched an eyebrow and offered a cocky grin. If there *was* such a thing as gaydar, it was whirling and flashing like a siren by now. Jamie would have bet money Tuck was gay, or at least bi.

Jamie stripped off his outer shirt, thought about but rejected the idea of taking off his thermal undershirt and turned his back to Tuck. In a moment, powerful warm fingers made contact with his shoulders, pressing gently at first, kneading the twisted, aching muscles.

"Man, you're hard as a rock," Tuck observed.

You referring to my neck or my cock? Jamie came that close to saying it out loud, but opted instead for, "That feels great. Don't stop." The strong, deep massage almost hurt, though at the same time it felt wonderful. Tuck moved in closer as he worked. He smelled good, like soap and pine needles. His touch was firm, but also sensual, the pads of his thick fingers gliding over Jamie's flesh, sending shivers of desire tingling down his spine.

How easy it would be to twist his head just a little and say, "Kiss me." Would Tuck respond? Something whispered inside Jamie that he would. He dared to lean lightly into the other man's touch.

"This isn't going to work." Tuck abruptly withdrew his hands. Jamie nearly cried out with dismay. Had he been completely off base about Tuck? Was he in fact as straight as an arrow? He bit his tongue and waited for Tuck to announce he couldn't massage a gay man.

He turned to face Tuck's decree. Tuck threw him off guard again with an enigmatic smile. "You're so tense, your muscles are tied in knots from your neck down. The minute I move from your shoulders to your neck, the muscles bunch up again. The only way this will work is if you lie down. We'll start at the base of your spine and work our way up. That's the best way to trick the muscles into relaxing fully."

Jamie stretched out eagerly, weak with relief to have his sudden hypothesis that Tuck was straight refuted, or at least not definitively proven. Tuck shifted beside him, his strong fingers gliding confidently over Jamie's back, easing the skittishness he felt both in body and mind. After a while Jamie felt himself drifting, sliding into a light doze, the blizzard just white noise in the background.

He came wide awake when Tuck's fingers moved beneath his T-shirt, sending electric sparks over Jamie's bare skin. Tuck pressed his palms flat against Jamie's back, stroking the flesh with a light, sensual touch. Jamie permitted himself a languorous sigh, imagining Tuck was his lover.

"That's better." Tuck's hands continued to roam over Jamie's back. "You were wound up tighter than a spring. You should be careful about holding that kind of tension in your body. It's not good for you."

"Mmph," Jamie managed, sinking blissfully into the cushions as Tuck worked his magic. His erection throbbed. Maybe he'd just roll over, unzip his jeans and complain of the tension building up in his cock. Would the altruistic Dr. Tucker take pity?

Tuck shifted and Jamie felt Tuck's weight settling on the backs of his thighs. "I can get at your neck better this way," Tuck offered. "Now that we've got your back muscles cooperating." He leaned forward, draping his hard body over Jamie's back.

That's when he felt it. The hard, unmistakable press of an erect cock against his lower back. *Jesus H. Christ.* Tuck was hot for him. His own cock responded, hardening to a painful degree. With the last six weeks of enforced celibacy, it seemed like forever since another man had touched him.

No straight guy would ever lean over like this for a

massage. No way, absolutely no way. For a moment Tuck didn't even pretend to massage him, his hands resting lightly on Jamie's shoulders, his cock still hard as ever against Jamie's lower back. Tuck's scent was in his nostrils, his warm, sweet breath at his neck. He could feel Tuck's heart tapping against him.

Jamie was afraid to move, afraid he might actually come in his pants if he did. Until this point, he'd held himself under tight rein, not permitting himself to feel the attraction that now rushed over him with the force of an Arctic gale.

He would just twist over beneath Tuck, let his shirt ride up as he shifted position and pulled Tuck down for the kiss he simply had to have...

"There's still no Internet...oh..."

Jamie startled at the sound of Brendan's voice. Tuck's hands jerked from beneath Jamie's shirt, the weight of his warm, heavy body suddenly withdrawn.

Jamie could hear the defensive fluster in Tuck's tone. "I—I was just giving Jamie a massage. He's really tense with this blizzard situation." Was he embarrassed at having been caught lying over another man, his hands beneath his shirt? Afraid Brendan might think he was, heaven forbid, *gay*? Or maybe the two were lovers, but so discreet even Jamie hadn't guessed.

Tuck's laugh sounded forced. "He was wound so tight I was afraid he was going to crack in half. Feeling better now, Jamie?"

Jamie rolled over, arranging his face into a neutral, bland smile. "Much, thanks. You have magic fingers." He watched as Tuck looked nervously toward Brendan, his face flushing. Jealousy poked Jamie like a poison dart. *Bastard. You were into me. I know you were.*

Ah well, if nothing else, Tuck had given him an excellent massage. He couldn't remember feeling so physically relaxed in months. Whatever there was or wasn't between Tuck and Brendan, he would probably never know. After all, this blizzard would blow over in a day or so, and they'd all head their separate ways.

Brendan knew his face was burning and cursed himself for it. Why was he reacting like this? What was it his business what Tuck and Jamie did? *Because it's Tuck, damn it,* his heart answered.

Brendan didn't consider himself gay. He'd had girlfriends, one of whom he'd nearly married. He'd thought he was in love with her but had finally come to the realization it would never work. He wanted more than she, or really any woman he'd ever been with, had been able to give him. He wanted passion. He wanted the kind of fierce, aching longing that probably only existed in love poems and corny movies.

He'd thought often over the past year about David Tucker and the intense connection he'd felt for him when they'd worked together the first time. In fact, he'd scared himself to death over his feelings, sensing the possibility of the passion and yearning he longed for, and then realizing it was for a *guy.*

He'd managed to put Tuck out of his mind for long stretches of time as the months passed, convincing himself it had been the combination of alcohol, close quarters and loneliness that had drawn him to another man.

But late at night, alone in his bed with only his hand and his fantasies for company, Tuck would slip into his mind, unbidden, even unwelcome, peering into Brendan's soul with those dark, serious eyes and whispering his deepest secrets.

The last six weeks had been a sweet kind of torture, or a tortured kind of sweetness, depending how one looked at it. Still unsure of his feelings or their implications for the way he defined himself as a man, he'd done nothing to let Tuck know he might be interested. Interested in what? He could barely allow himself to imagine, much less articulate, what.

How ironic to be stranded now with him, all but Jamie out of the picture, only to find those two in some kind of embrace, Jamie's shirt bunched up, Tuck clearly embarrassed at whatever had been going on.

Brendan banished his unanswered questions and confusion to a dark corner of his brain. He decided to act as if he hadn't stumbled on anything untoward. The wind rattling the building recalled him to the seriousness of their situation.

"I was saying we still don't have Internet or cell phone service. It's possible the dish was knocked over or even blown away or something. With these shifting winds, we might be able to get a window or door open eventually. Then we can clear some of that snow away and assess the damage."

Tuck, who had walked over to one of the windows, lifted the insulated flap and stared into the gray, whipping wilderness beyond. "These Antarctic blizzards can last up to a week or longer. We might as well relax until it passes. Once the winds die down, we should be able to get a better handle on the situation."

"So you think it could be as long as a week?" Jamie had risen from the sofa and was tucking his shirt back into his pants. He was a good-looking guy, tall and strong like Tuck. He had light brown hair, a little shaggy around the ears at the moment, with bangs that fell into his very blue eyes on a regular basis. Brendan had wondered sometimes how Jamie could work, bent over his bench in the lab, his hair falling into his face, but he got results. He was bright, a good worker and had a wry, quick sense of humor.

He looked young—he *was* young—and clearly anxious over

the situation in which they found themselves. Brendan could hear the forced calm in his tone and his heart went out to Jamie. Maybe Tuck really had just been giving him a friendly massage.

Not wanting to go there again in his head, Brendan moved toward his own bed. "I know it's kind of early in the day, but anyone want some scotch? George Lawrence left me this bottle. I don't know about you two, but I could use a drink."

"Hey." Tuck laughed. "It's five o'clock somewhere."

Chapter Three

Tuck opened his eyes and closed his mouth. He lifted his head, which had been lolling uncomfortably against his neck. Disoriented, he looked down to see Jamie asleep, his head resting on Tuck's outstretched legs. Brendan was nowhere to be seen.

They'd made themselves some lunch—several cans of beef vegetable soup and some crackers, plus the remains of the spaghetti from the night before. Along with the meal, they'd all had quite a bit to drink, especially Jamie, who was still out like a light.

Tuck didn't remember falling asleep. He did remember their conversation, which started out soberly discussing what they would need to do in order to ride out the storm. They agreed to shut down the labs and storage rooms completely to conserve fuel. Limited washing up, so as not to tax the hot water heater, and limited cooking to conserve the propane. Luckily they had several boxes of hot and cold cereal, energy bars, peanut butter, crackers and canned soups and vegetables, as well as about thirty gallons of purified water in the pantry. Once the storm abated, they would try to get outside, clear away some of the snow and check out the satellite dish.

When the meal was over, bottle in hand, they'd moved to the sleeping quarters to relax. Jamie had joined Tuck on the couch. Brendan sat on the cot next to it, eventually stretching out, his arms behind his head, the bottle of scotch on the floor beside him.

As they continued to talk and drink, it seemed to Tuck that Brendan was avoiding his eye, mostly staring at the ceiling. Tuck was dying to know exactly what Brendan had witnessed between Jamie and himself. Was he avoiding Tuck's eye because he disapproved? Or was there something else at play?

Tuck still wasn't quite sure what had gone on himself. His initial intention had been to calm the obviously anxious Jamie. It was also a diversion to focus on Jamie's knotted muscles. Tuck had always enjoyed giving massages, deriving satisfaction as tight muscles responded to his skilled touch, easing and untwisting beneath his fingers.

So caught up with his research and his obsession with Brendan, he'd never really paid much attention to Jamie before, at least not sexually. They'd known each other from the institute back home, but only professionally. Jamie had only been there a year and kept pretty much to himself. During these past weeks in Antarctica, they had a cordial, positive relationship in the lab, but had had little personal interaction.

At first he was unprepared for the strong sexual reaction he experienced once he touched Jamie's firmly muscled back and neck, but in retrospect he shouldn't have been. Jamie was, after all, extremely good looking. He was funny and smart, though a little younger than Tuck was used to considering as potential partner material.

Even back in Monterey he'd suspected Jamie might be gay, and the massage had done nothing to dispel this feeling. A straight guy wouldn't have let Tuck touch him the way he had, slipping his hands beneath Jamie's shirt and most especially, lying over him, allowing Jamie to feel the bulge of his erection.

How far would it have gone if Brendan hadn't chosen that moment to poke his head around the door?

He smiled down at the sleeping Jamie. With a light touch, he pushed Jamie's flopping bangs from his face, though they promptly fell back again. Jamie was seven years younger than Tuck's thirty-two, and in repose he appeared even younger. Did he have someone at home worrying about him now? His parents, a roommate, a lover?

Jamie stirred, turning his head so his nose rested on Tuck's fly. Tuck's cock rose in response, like Pavlov's dog hearing the bell. Embarrassed, even though Jamie was ostensibly still sleeping, Tuck moved away, letting Jamie's head fall to the mattress.

Jamie opened his eyes and lifted his head, unfocused blue eyes coming to rest on Tuck's face. Pulling himself into a sitting position, he stretched his arms overhead and yawned. "Man, I fell asleep."

"Me too." Tuck surreptitiously admired the other man's broad chest. "Guess we're not used to drinking half a bottle of whiskey in the middle of the day."

"I guess not." Jamie smiled. His eyes were almond-shaped and slightly slanted beneath prominent cheekbones, lending him an exotic appearance. His mouth was sensuous, the lips plump and inviting.

Jamie eyed Tuck with a quizzical expression. Without speaking, he touched Tuck's thigh with three fingers. Tuck looked at his hand and back up into Jamie's face. There was a question in Jamie's eyes, mixed with the unmistakable smolder of desire.

Jamie leaned forward, his eyes still locked on Tuck's. Tuck found himself drawn toward Jamie by a powerful force. They moved in slow motion until their lips were touching.

Jamie's hand still rested on Tuck's thigh. For several seconds they remained still, lips pressed together, hearts beating. A part of Tuck didn't believe it was happening. He was drunk and dreaming. He would wake in a minute, alone on his cot as usual.

Jamie parted his lips, his tongue licking along Tuck's mouth, nudging until Tuck let it gain entrance. Tentatively Tuck explored his mouth in return. Jamie tasted faintly of whiskey and peppermint. Jamie clutched at Tuck's thigh and placed his other hand on the back of Tuck's neck.

Tuck's eyes were open, focused on the door that led to the kitchen. He could hear the faint tap-tapping of Brendan's fingers on his keyboard. What would Brendan think if he walked into the room? Did it matter? Brendan was straight. He'd made his interest, or rather lack thereof, pretty clear since the one, sexually charged interaction the year before.

And here was Jamie, handsome, sexy and obviously interested. It was a relief to have something to distract himself from the constant underlying anxiety caused by their being stranded and without communication with the outside world.

Abandoning himself to the moment, he responded ardently to Jamie's kiss, pulling him close and running his hands over Jamie's back and shoulders as their tongues collided. Jamie drew back long enough to grip Tuck's shoulders and push him down against the sofa.

Clambering over him, Jamie again sought his mouth, catching Tuck's lower lip between his teeth. Tuck could feel Jamie's erection, hard as steel against him. Tuck's balls were tight with need, the desire he'd been harboring so long for Brendan transferring itself to the hard-bodied man lying on top of him.

He brought his arms around Jamie and slipped his hands

into Jamie's jeans, pushing past the elastic of his underwear to cup the muscular globes of his ass. Jamie shuddered and moaned.

"Jesus," Jamie hissed, drawing out the second syllable in a sibilant breath. He buried his head between Tuck's head and shoulder. Tuck could feel Jamie's heart beating violently. He could feel Jamie's tongue, wet and warm against his neck, his cock thrusting and grinding against Tuck's hipbone.

Jamie's breath quickened to a rapid pant, his body suddenly spasming on top of Tuck's. Jamie emitted a small, guttural cry. There were too many layers of clothing between them for him to feel the spurt, but he knew from Jamie's limp, heavy weight upon him that Jamie had come in his pants.

Tuck's cock still throbbed, trapped in his clothing, pinned under Jamie's strong body. He held onto Jamie like a lifeline, confusion rising beneath the lingering lust. What was he doing, seducing this sweet, sexy young guy with Brendan in the next room? Was this new attraction purely a result of the dire straits in which they found themselves?

Or was Tuck now falling for not one guy but two?

"Fuck." Jamie rolled from the cot to the floor. "I didn't mean to—" His face twisted into a sheepish grin. "You're just so damn hot, and it's been so long..." Jamie looked from Tuck to the closed kitchen door and back again. "Listen, let me return the favor."

"No, we're cool." In fact, Tuck felt anything but cool. He, too, looked toward the kitchen, straining to hear the sound of the keyboard on the other side of the door. Not that they'd done anything wrong, but he really didn't need Brendan walking in on them again.

He glanced at Jamie, still sprawled on the floor beside the cot. "Maybe you want to, uh, clean up a little." He gestured with his chin toward Jamie's crotch, where a small stain was spreading along the fly.

Flushing, Jamie jumped up and headed toward his own cot. Grabbing some clothing from the trunk at the end of it, he went into the bathroom, shutting the door behind him.

Tuck put his hands behind his head and stared at the ceiling. His own cock was still hard as iron but he found himself too distracted to do anything about it. His mind was jumping from Jamie to Brendan like oil sizzling in a pan. What the hell had just happened? What did he think he was doing?

I haven't the slightest fucking idea, he answered himself.

Earlier, Brendan had awoken before the other two, alone on the cot. For a long moment he'd looked at the two sleeping men, Tucker slumped uncomfortably against the sofa back, Jamie's head on his lap like a child.

He had wanted to push Jamie away. To lay Tuck down and put a pillow beneath his head. He wanted to lie beside him and sleep—just sleep, neither of them stirring until the storm had ended and rescuers were on their way.

Brendan's head hurt, his mouth tasted sour and his bladder was full. He hauled himself up from the cot and went into the bathroom to relieve himself.

When he returned to the sleeping quarters, neither man had moved, both still caught in the net of an alcohol-induced stupor. Brendan, though shorter and slighter than either of them, obviously could hold his liquor better. This thought amused him and at the same time made him feel old. Not that he was much older than Tuck. Yet sometimes Brendan felt like an old man already—set in his ways, a lonely guy who never took risks. At least not risks of the heart.

With a sigh, he left the two sleeping beauties and sat in the kitchen to work on some reports. He closed the door between the two rooms so his typing wouldn't disturb them, realizing belatedly that this was rather silly, as the wind still whined and moaned outside, coupled with the sound of hail tapping insistently on the roof and buffeting the walls.

He'd actually managed to distract himself with his work, even forgetting for stretches at a time where they were and what was happening outside their snug abode. After a while he'd heard Tuck and Jamie stirring and talking quietly. He expected them to poke their heads into the kitchen. When that didn't happen right away, he forced himself to continue with his work.

In time he did become involved again in what he was doing. When he finished a thought, he realized the murmuring had stopped. The silence made him wonder if they'd fallen back asleep.

He stood and moved toward the door that separated them. He turned the knob, opening the door only a few inches when he heard them—the sound of the sofa springs creaking, a muffled moan, rapid breathing and then a small, animal cry of lust.

He felt in his bones what he was hearing even before his brain caught up. Feeling as if someone had dumped a bucket of ice water over his head, he jerked the door shut and sagged heavily against it, his heart hammering painfully.

He wasn't sure how long he leaned there, his mind blank, his heart thudding. All he knew was he felt more alone than at any other time in his life.

After a minute, an hour, a lifetime, he heard the sound of Tuck's open, sunny laugh and was seized with an overwhelming desire to see Tuck, even if he were naked in Jamie's arms. Without giving himself a chance to fully consider what he was doing, he pushed the door open. To his immense relief, he saw Tuck was alone.

At the sound of the opening door, Tuck looked up to see Brendan leaning against the doorframe. "Tuck. We have to talk."

Any number of scenarios passed through Tuck's mind, running the gamut from het outrage to the admission of secret love and jealous longing. Brendan remained in the door so Tuck stood, glad his lingering erection was hidden beneath his flannel shirt. He moved to follow Brendan into the kitchen, Jamie all but forgotten.

Sitting caddy-corner from Brendan at the head of the long table, he waited for whatever it was Brendan had to say. Beside Brendan's laptop was the nearly empty bottle of whiskey and a small juice glass.

"May I?"

Brendan nodded, pushing the bottle toward him. "I'll join you." He went to the cabinet and returned a moment later with a second glass. Tuck poured a few fingers for each of them, lifted his own and drank it in a single burning gulp.

Brendan sipped his and set it back on the table. "I've checked the supply logs." His tone was brisk and businesslike. Was it only Tuck's imagination, or did something more urgent lurk just beneath it? "I did a few calculations, based on our discussion about shutting down the labs and supplying heat and electricity only to the living quarters. If we set the temperature at sixty, limit the use of the propane stove and keep water usage to a minimum, we can easily survive for two to three weeks. We have enough food and water for longer than that."

Thoughts of any amorous admission on Brendan's part rapidly receded in the face of his words. "Two to three *weeks*. Do you really think this storm's going to last that long?"

"No. I hope not. The only thing that worries me"—Brendan lowered his voice, glancing toward the sleeping quarters—"is how close we are to the winter season. If the winds keep up, it won't be safe to land a plane. There's a possibility, though an unlikely one, that we could be stuck here through the winter. But even if that did happen, they'd more than likely be able to parachute supplies to us. We aren't going to starve. We aren't going to die. We just have to conserve energy and supplies and be sensible."

Tuck swallowed, absorbing the possibility of spending the winter stranded in an Antarctic wasteland, with only wood, steel and insulated fabric between them and the harsh elements. He knew the temperature outside could drop as low as -50°C, the blizzards reducing the visibility to just a few meters, with the added specter of twenty-four-hour darkness for one hundred and five days when the sun dipped permanently below the horizon.

He'd read of the terror that could overcome men trapped in this kind of situation, blackness falling over an outer world of icy desolation, an inner world of despair. He picked up the bottle, horrified to see his hand shaking as he poured.

Brendan placed his hand over Tuck's and squeezed. When he spoke, his voice was gentle. "It's okay, Tuck. We're gonna be okay. I promise."

Tuck looked gratefully at Brendan, desperately wanting to believe him. His heart clutched as he lost himself in those gray green eyes. He looked down at Brendan's hand, the fingers long and slender over his own larger hand, the skin pale in contrast to his.

Brendan, following his gaze, snatched his hand away, his face flushing to a dull red. He drank the rest of his whiskey in a gulp and set the glass down with a thunk against the wood.

Is this how it'll always be? Tuck wondered with something near despair. *Each of us dancing on the edge of our emotions, neither with the courage to confront the other or even our own feelings?*

Maybe if he said something, anything, to let Brendan know how much he cared. Maybe all Brendan needed was an opening, some gentle coaxing, to rekindle the magic they'd once shared, however briefly.

Tuck poured himself another inch of whiskey and drank half. In a strange way he was grateful for the blizzard, grateful for the reprieve from the very real probability of losing Brendan again. Now at least he had a chance to make his feelings known, something he should have done at the outset of the project.

And then there was Jamie. What the hell had just happened back there? They couldn't seem to be alone for more than a minute without groping each other. Where did Jamie fit into this erotic stew of confusion?

He stared down at the amber liquid, trying to frame what he wanted to say to Brendan. He didn't want to pressure him, or embarrass him any more than he already seemed to be. He just wanted Brendan to know how he felt. He *needed* him to know.

"Brendan, I have something to—" he began.

"It's okay," Brendan cut him off, jumping up from the table. "It's none of my business."

Momentarily confused by the unexpected response, Tuck paused. A noise behind them distracted him and he turned to see.

"Hey, there you are." Jamie, in fresh jeans, wearing a grin on his handsome face, looked from Brendan to Tuck and then at the bottle of whiskey sitting between them on the table. "Am I missing the party?"

Brendan stared down at his hands, realizing he was holding the back of the chair in a white-knuckled grip. Letting go, he sat, forcing himself to be calm and rational. He surveyed the two men, wondering if this was when they'd tell him they were involved in a homosexual affair. How would he react? Nonchalant? Outraged? Jealous? He honestly didn't know. Seeing Jamie eye the bottle, he rose and retrieved another juice glass from the cabinet.

"If we're going to be here more than a few days," Tuck observed, "maybe we better ration what's left." There were only a few inches of liquor left in the bottle.

Jamie smiled slyly. "Happily, that won't be necessary."

"Why's that?" Tuck turned toward him. Brendan saw something flash between them—the secret understanding of...no, he refused to even think it. He looked away.

Jamie continued. "On the bottom shelf of the pantry in the far right corner there's a box. Inside that box is a special stash. Gordon told me about it—ten bottles of liquor—scotch, vodka, gin, tequila, all kinds of stuff. Said he was leaving it for next spring, when the project resumes. He swore me to secrecy. But I think, under the circumstances, he would forgive us if we, uh, borrowed a bit. We can always buy more later, when we get back to the States..."

The last words seemed to catch and die in Jamie's throat. The roar of the gale outside, which until that moment had almost faded into white noise, seemed to magnify, its howl

38

menacing.

They were all quiet, listening to the sounds of a tempest raging. Both Tuck and Jamie looked tense. Jamie especially had a wild look in his eyes. Brendan forgot his self-absorbed pondering. He was the lab team leader, the oldest and the most experienced field scientist of the three. Whatever his own personal longings and confusion, he needed to rise to the occasion and offer what support and comfort he could to the others.

"I'm sure he'll forgive us." Brendan smiled at Jamie. "Why don't you select our next bottle of poison?" Turning to Tuck, he added, "How about a game of cards?"

Chapter Four

Jamie found a bottle of vodka and brought it to the table. He was grateful to Brendan for pulling him back from the brink. Faced with the stark realization they might *not* make it back to the States, he'd very nearly lost it.

If he'd had his choice, he would rather climb into the one of the beds with Tuck and just have sex until they were rescued, but with Brendan around that wasn't much of a possibility.

Or was it?

He wiped out the juice glasses with a paper towel and set them in a neat row beside the bottle. He watched Brendan shutting down his laptop and sliding it into its case and recalled the look of longing he'd seen Tuck flash Brendan's way the night before. Was something there? Was it only on Tuck's side, or was it returned? Was Brendan one of those bi-curious guys, the type who could be drawn out with some liquor and patience?

The thought intrigued him. Imagine the fun they could have if two became three. He could barely suppress an evil grin at the thought of all the delicious possibilities and combinations.

Tuck retrieved the cards and returned to the table. He began to shuffle the deck. Brendan was watching him. None of them had showered or shaved that morning, in their effort to conserve water and fuel. A sexy blond stubble showed on Brendan's jaw and cheek. Jamie's cock ached with appreciation.

"What should we play?" Tuck asked. "Not gin. Jamie's too damn good at remembering every card."

Jamie had a better idea. "Let's play Blackjack. Only let's spice it up a little. Blackjack Truth or Dare. Except instead of a dare, if you don't answer the question, you have to drink a shot of vodka. We'll play face up, since we're not betting. Whoever wins gets to ask the question to whoever he wants."

"Oh, I don't know—" Brendan began, his voice wary.

"Sounds like fun," Tuck interjected eagerly. "Come on, Brendan. You chicken? Got some secrets in that closet of yours you don't want us to know about?"

Brendan flushed and Jamie held his breath, waiting for Brendan to nix the idea. To his surprised delight, Brendan flashed one of his gorgeous smiles. "What the hell. Let the games begin."

Tuck dealt two initial cards to each player. Jamie had a ten and a five, Tuck a three and a seven, Brendan a king and a two. "Jamie?" Tuck nodded toward him.

"Hit me." Jamie tapped his cards. Tuck dealt him another five.

"Not bad." Tuck frowned appreciatively.

Jamie put a hand over his cards. "I'll stand."

Tuck turned toward Brendan, who nodded. Tuck dealt him a nine. "Whoa, twenty-one in the first hand. Way to go, Brendan."

"Pure luck." Brendan shrugged but looked pleased.

Tuck dealt himself a two. "Twelve. I'm feeling lucky. Let's see what I get." He flipped over another card. It was a queen.

"Busted. So Brendan gets to ask the question, right?"

"Yep." Jamie nodded, curious who and what Brendan would ask.

"Since Tuck lost, we'll start with him." Brendan shifted so he was facing Tuck and seemed to ponder the question. "Okay. How old were you when you lost your virginity?"

"That's easy. I was seventeen. It was in the back of my parents' car with a girl I'd been dating for a few months. It was basically a disaster."

"Details," Jamie blurted, intrigued. Was Tuck truly bisexual or had he just been experimenting with a woman, as so many gay guys did before they recognized or felt free enough to admit their true orientation?

"Hey, you're not asking the questions." Tuck laughed. "Asked and answered. Let's play another round."

"Oh, come on," Brendan urged, surprising Jamie. "Tell us the details."

Tuck poured a shot of vodka into his glass. "Okay, but I'll need this to get me through it." They laughed and Jamie found himself relaxing for the first time since Tuck had held him in his arms. Even the wind outside seemed calmer. Tuck tossed back the alcohol, winced and shuddered. "That's rough." He made a face.

"Bet the second one will taste better," Brendan offered.

"And the third one even better," Jamie added.

Tuck grinned and leaned back in his chair. "Okay. You guys sure you want to hear this?"

"Quit stalling," Jamie teased.

"Okay, okay. Let's see. It was the dreaded senior prom. The dance was in full swing. We slipped out to the parking lot to smoke some weed. She produced a condom from her purse and said, 'Happy anniversary.' We'd been going out six months or something and we'd yet to go all the way. I wasn't terribly excited about the idea of my first time happening in the back of a car, but on the other hand, I was seventeen and being offered the chance to lose my virginity. So I seized the moment, as they say.

"It was kind of awkward. She was wearing this evening gown thing with lots of extra slips and stuff, but we finally got it hoisted up around her waist. She had on stockings and a garter belt, I remember that. I was in a rented tuxedo of some color not found in nature. We kind of made out for a while and groped each other. I must have made it in about one inch and then I came. It was all over in like three seconds."

Jamie shook his head and Brendan laughed. "Wow, that's even worse than my first time."

Tuck grinned. "We'll have to find out about that. I'll deal another round." He dealt the cards and this time Brendan came up the loser and Tuck the winner. Tuck, predictably, turned to Brendan. "Okay. So tell us. When and how did Dr. Brendan Aaronson lose his virginity?"

Jamie expected Brendan to hem and haw, but he launched right in. "I was barely nineteen. She was twenty-two."

"An older woman." Jamie raised his eyebrows.

"Yep. She was a grad student. I was a freshman. She was tutoring me in French and well, one thing led to another and I found myself in her bed. We weren't lovers, we weren't in love, but she was eager and I was a nineteen-year-old guy, which of course is synonymous with horny. I probably lasted a full three minutes longer than Tuck, though."

Tuck dealt another round, and as if it were planned, this time Jamie lost. Tuck was again the winner and he turned to Jamie. "Okay. Your turn. Spill the beans."

Jamie hesitated. Did they really want the truth? Obviously Tuck could handle it, but what about Brendan? What the hell. What was life without risk?

"His name was Jordan. I was eighteen. He was twenty." He stared at Brendan, daring him to react. He couldn't read Brendan's expression. He glanced at Tuck, who nodded and smiled encouragingly. "We'd been hanging around together for a while. I met him at school—he lived on my floor in the dorms. He had his own room and I had the roommate from hell, so I was always in his room.

"It started in that most typical of ways—a back massage." He glanced at Tuck, who was, he saw, watching Brendan. What was it between them? Closing his eyes, he forced himself to focus on his memories. He hadn't thought about Jordan Decker in a while. Jordan had gone to Africa the semester after they met to do volunteer work and Jamie had lost touch with him.

"It was my freshman year. I hadn't come out at that point. That is, I knew I was gay, but I hadn't told anyone. He was openly gay. I mean, flamingly flamboyant." Jamie laughed at the memory of his eccentric first lover. "He wore the most amazing getups. He would shop at the thrift stores and show up in red plaid pants, a white silk pirate's shirt, a long, brightly painted scarf slung over his shoulder, black boots and a fedora. He managed to pull it off, though. I was always in my uniform of a T-shirt and jeans. I guess we were a strange couple, but it worked for us.

"He introduced me to all the delights of male-male sex. He was slow, deliberate and gentle. I was really lucky, in retrospect. He was a great lover. I nearly failed that semester, though, as I recall." He laughed and was pleased to note not only Tuck, but Brendan laughed with him.

"To first times." Tuck poured them each a shot. Jamie

drank and grimaced. Tuck was right—it was pretty vile, with no crushed ice and orange juice to mask the taste of the pure grain alcohol, but the accompanying warmth spreading quickly through his bloodstream made up for it.

He closed his eyes, remembering. Jordan used to suck his cock for hours, drawing him nearly to climax over and over. Jamie spent every spare moment naked on Jordan's bed, his cock in Jordan's hot, eager mouth.

It was several weeks before they worked their way toward anal intercourse. Jordan was a top, never on the receiving end of anal sex. This was okay with Jamie, especially as Jordan kept him on the edge of orgasm for so long that by the time Jordan had lubricated and entered Jamie, it only took a few strokes with fingers and cock to make him shoot everything he had. Over time he came not only to tolerate, but to crave the penetrating invasion of Jordan's cock snaking its way inside him.

"I'm hungry." Tuck cut into Jamie's musings. "What time is it, anyway?"

Brendan looked at his watch. "It's seven fifteen already. How time flies when you're having fun." His tone was dry, a sardonic grin on his face. "How about something extravagant, like more canned soup and some peanut butter on a spoon? We ate the last of the crackers at lunch."

Jamie giggled and realized he was drunk again—for the second time in a day. Not that he had any particular reason to want to remain sober. If marathon sex wasn't in the offing, maybe a weeklong binge, or however long it took for the weather to abate, was the next best option.

After dinner they decided to continue their card game in the sleeping quarters. "Let's put our quilts around one of the space heaters," Tuck suggested.

"Hey, cool." Jamie moved toward the light switch. "We'll turn off the lights. It'll be like a campfire."

Brendan glanced sharply toward Tuck, who met his gaze. Was he recalling that night as well?

They settled around the space heater, which cast a red light over them, softening and suffusing as it radiated through the room. Jamie poured them each more vodka while Tuck shuffled and dealt the cards.

Jamie won the first round. "My question is for Brendan. Remember, you have to answer the question and be truthful, or drink a shot."

It was evident to Brendan from the slur in his speech that Jamie was pretty drunk. But then, they all were, as they'd been drinking most of the day. He stretched out, leaning up on one elbow so his head was near Tuck's thigh. Tuck sat on crossed legs caddy-corner to him, with Jamie on the other side of the heater.

"Okay, shoot."

"Have you ever fantasized about being with a guy?"

Brendan felt his face heat, though he'd expected something along these lines. Briefly he considered refusing to answer and drinking the liquor instead, though he knew he'd had enough. He glanced at Tuck, who was watching him with those soulful eyes.

"Yeah, I guess I have."

"You *guess*?" Jamie laughed.

"I answered the question. Time to move on. Deal us another round, Tuck."

"Hey, no fair," Jamie interjected. He too had stretched out along his quilt.

"What's not fair about it? You asked, I answered."

"These scientist types are slippery," Tuck joked. "You can't put anything over on them."

He dealt another round. This time Brendan won. The liquor had loosened his tongue. He decided to ask the same question of Tuck. "What about you, Dr. Tucker? Ever fantasized about being with a guy?"

"He's done more than fantasize," Jamie chortled. In the uncomfortable silence that followed, he added, "Man, I'm smashed. We're gonna have serious hangovers in the morning." He punctuated his remark with a loud slurp from his juice glass.

Tuck looked embarrassed. Brendan cursed himself for asking the question. For a moment he'd actually forgotten the guilty pulling apart from what Tuck claimed was just a massage, and then later the muffled, telltale sounds of sex behind the door. Jamie might be drunk, but Brendan decided he himself wasn't drunk enough.

"Gimme more a' that." He waved his empty juice glass in Tuck's direction. Tuck poured from the bottle, which was already nearly two-thirds empty. The question hung unanswered in the air—too late to take it back.

Tuck answered. "Um. Yeah. I have. Yes." Brendan glanced at Jamie. He was lying flat on his back now, his eyes closed, his hands clasped loosely over his flannel-covered chest. His lips lifted and curled into a grin at Tuck's response. Brendan felt a sudden nearly overwhelming urge to wipe that knowing smile away.

Jesus, what was wrong with him? Was he jealous of them? Of Jamie for already having what, or rather who, he wanted? He turned to Tuck, who was watching him, his expression beseeching.

"What? What is it, Tuck?"

"You," Tuck mouthed.

"Me?"

Tuck nodded, clutching the vodka bottle. They were all hiding behind and in the alcohol, Brendan realized. So where was the courage that was supposed to come along with the buzz?

A soft snore issued from Jamie's lips. Tuck and Brendan looked at each other and smiled. Tuck leaned over Jamie, brushing his long bangs from his face. The easy intimacy of the gesture at once moved and hurt Brendan, adding to his emotional turmoil.

Tuck drank deeply from his juice glass and let it tumble to the floor beside him. Screwing the cap into place, he pushed the bottle aside. He held his hands out to the glowing heater. "It's like before," he whispered. "Do you remember? Last summer. The campfire?"

Did he remember? Brendan had relived every moment of that night at least a hundred times in his head, no matter how many times he'd tried to forget it. They'd sat so close they might have been on each other's laps. Tuck's strong thigh had pressed against his own, their hands shifting over denim, pretending it was an accident each time they touched. Then Tuck's comforting arm around his shoulders, holding him close, making him feel safe and warm. His skin had burned for days with the memory of Tuck's touch, his heart aching with a longing he'd refused to permit himself to acknowledge.

"Yeah. I remember."

Tuck shifted until he was lying down, his head close to Brendan's, his body perpendicular. Brendan's arm was sprawled out by his side. He stared up at the ceiling, softly illuminated by the heater. The unforgiving storm continued to pummel the dwelling, but they were, for now at least, safe and secure inside.

Brendan wanted to talk more about last summer, about whatever it was that had gone on between them, if anything at all. But first he had to know if there was something between Tuck and Jamie. His eyes fixed on the ceiling, he dared, "What's going on between you two? The truth."

There was a long silence. Brendan closed his eyes and waited, willing his mind to go blank. Finally Tuck answered. "I don't know. It just kind of happened. I guess I've been aware in the back of my mind that he's gay. We work together back in California, you know. He always kept to himself both there and here, so it never occurred to me before to...I don't know. I was just so focused on you—"

Tuck drew in a sudden breath, his last words hanging in the air like a bubble that, if Brendan reacted, would burst and disappear. He said nothing, waiting. Tuck blew out the breath and continued, letting the bubble pop.

"Today it started with me trying to comfort him. He was so keyed up I thought he was going to jump out of his skin. You know, he's a seriously good-looking guy. I guess things just progressed from there."

"I heard something. I heard sounds when I was in the kitchen—" Brendan cut himself off, embarrassed.

"Oh. Yeah. Um...well, yeah. I guess something kind of happened. I mean, but not, you know, like out-and-out sex. We, uh, we kissed. We fondled."

Tuck offered no further details, nor was it, Brendan knew, any of his business. He tried to come to terms with his conflicting feelings. One part jealousy, one part hetero indignation at the thought of two gay guys groping each other in the next room, one part arousal at the very same thought.

Throw in sexual desire for not only Tuck but now for Jamie as well and Brendan realized he didn't know what the hell he was thinking or feeling.

It was possible they wouldn't be rescued. They all knew it, even if none had so far voiced it in such stark terms. There was a chance the blizzard would rage so long it would be too late. Winter, with its perennial darkness and howling winds, would settle over them like a shroud.

He might die without finding out just what and who he really was. If his feelings had been meteorological in nature, they would have conjured a tornado to rival the storm outside.

He did know he liked lying beside Tuck. There was an easiness to it, no doubt fueled by vodka, but nevertheless, he felt good just being near him. Tuck touched Brendan's arm and despite the layers of fabric between them, a shiver of desire moved through Brendan from Tuck's fingers.

A funny thought entered his head and because he was drunk, he said it out loud. "We're like those Colonial people, you know, when couples were courting and they wrapped them all up, fully clothed and swathed in blankets and put them in bed together to ensure no sexual contact?"

"Bundling," Tuck answered. "A strange ritual, to be sure." Tuck sat up and began to unbutton his shirt. "It's plenty warm by this heater. Take off your outer shirt, why don't you?"

Brendan sat, a sudden dizziness assailing him. With fumbling fingers, he managed to unbutton his shirt and push it from his shoulders. He looked over at Jamie, who hadn't moved, his chest rising and falling in the deep, slow rhythm of sleep. He looked back at Tuck, who had already removed his flannel shirt. Tuck's undershirt was black and molded to his broad, strong shoulders and muscular chest. Brendan realized he was staring and turned away. He also realized he had a hard-on, sprung to full life in his trousers.

He lay back down, turning his body slightly away, in case Tuck had witnessed his erection. Tuck, too, lay down. He squeezed Brendan's forearm. Brendan held himself still, unsure what was happening or what he was ready to have happen.

"Brendan." Tuck's voice was low. "You should know something. Ever since last summer, I've thought about you a lot. It was such a crazy coincidence to get tapped for this project and then find out you were on it too."

"Yeah. That was a coincidence all right."

"I'm glad we reconnected. This is going to sound nuts, but in a way I'm glad for this blizzard. I mean, you know, if it means we can finally find out. If there is anything to find out...about us. About, you know...things between us..."

Hope flared in Brendan like a warm, sparkling light. Yes, Tuck had admitted there was something with Jamie, but it was clear there was also something between them, between Tuck and himself, something Tuck seemed as eager to explore as he did.

They turned toward each other and scooted closer until their faces were nearly touching, their heads creating the point atop a triangle of which their bodies formed the two sides. Brendan's heart was jerking like a rubber ball bouncing against the walls of his rib cage, his lips tingling and aching in anticipation.

Oh Jesus, he's going to kiss me. He's going to kiss me. Brendan closed his eyes, surrendering himself to the whirl caused by the alcohol and the thrumming in his blood.

"You're trembling." Tuck's voice was gentle, concerned. "You okay?"

Brendan opened his eyes. "I don't know. I've never done this. And Jamie..."

Tuck twisted his head toward the sleeping man. "Dead to the world." He turned back. "Maybe we should get off this floor."

"Yeah." Brendan was at once deflated and relieved by the reprieve. They both got to their feet. Tuck held out his arms and Brendan moved into them. The embrace brought air to a gasping emptiness somewhere inside him. He leaned his head against Tuck's chest, all thoughts quieting at last.

Without planning it, as if it were the most natural thing in the world, he lifted his head and closed his eyes, his heart near to bursting as Tuck's lips touched his.

Chapter Five

The kiss was brief, closed lips brushing against one another. "Your heart's beating so fast," Tuck murmured. His own heart was smashing against his ribs and he literally felt weak in the knees. *Slow down, slow down,* he warned himself.

His balls were aching, his cock straining hard against the confines of his clothing. If he didn't get a little distance between them, he knew he was going to tear Brendan's clothes from his body and take him then and there.

Tuck hoped his voice portrayed a calm he didn't feel. "Let's lie down. We can push two of the cots together." The cots had heavy-duty wood frames with a thick mattress pad over the canvas set low to the ground. They were actually quite comfortable. Together they shoved the closest cot until it was touching Tuck's, which was flush against the wall. Retrieving their blankets, Tuck placed one across the makeshift double bed. Brendan sat on the edge, looking toward the inert figure of Jamie.

"You think he'll be okay down there? Should we wake him and have him get into his own bed?"

The last thing Tuck wanted was for Jamie to wake up. Not now. "He'll be fine. We'll keep an eye on him." He walked over to Jamie and pushed the space heater several feet from him so he wouldn't inadvertently knock it over if he moved in his sleep.

Returning to the bed, he sat beside Brendan. He reminded himself Brendan must be even more nervous than he was. "Let's lie down," he urged. He pushed at Brendan's shoulder, maneuvering himself so Brendan was nearest the wall.

Brendan lay on his side, facing Tuck. Tuck eased toward him, feeling in a way as if he were dealing with a wild animal, one he desperately didn't want to frighten away. He shifted until their bodies were touching at the shoulder, the groin, the thigh. He could feel Brendan's heart pounding.

Cautiously he brought a hand to Brendan's cheek. Brendan sucked in his breath, his eyes trained on Tuck's face. "Tuck. I don't know...I've never..."

"It's okay. You don't have to know. You don't have to do anything. It's just us. You and me. Please, Brendan. Just trust your instincts."

Tuck knew Brendan was scared, but he could feel the bulge of his erection, which matched Tuck's own. He hadn't pulled away when Tuck had dared to touch his arm before. And when they'd held one another, yes, it was the embrace of friends, but more, much more, had silently passed between them.

When Brendan had lifted his face, his eyes closed, the dark blond lashes brushing his cheekbones, offering a mouth made for plundering, Tuck had nearly gone out of his mind. It had taken every ounce of self-control to stop himself from crushing Brendan to his chest, forcing Brendan's lips apart with his tongue, claiming his mouth and in short order, his body.

Brendan might be protesting with his words, but he hadn't resisted. He was facing Tuck, allowing him to stroke his cheek. His eyes were closed, his hand resting on his hip. The bulge at his crotch was undeniable. *I've seen that cock, that sexy, long, thick cock,* Tuck thought, flashing back to the naked man in the shower.

Unable to resist a moment longer, he brought his face close to Brendan's. He touched Brendan's lips lightly with his own, as before. A brushing of skin, a testing of the waters. Brendan lifted his chin in silent collusion.

Pent-up longing spilled over, rendering Tuck suddenly reckless. He parted his lips, pressing his tongue into Brendan's mouth. Brendan jerked back with a gasp. Tuck reached for him, pulling his body hard against his own.

He slipped his hand to the nape of Brendan's neck, palming the back of his head while he kissed him. Brendan held himself stiffly, pushing against Tuck's tight embrace, though without much conviction. Tuck knew he was moving too fast. He couldn't help it. He didn't care. His tongue danced in Brendan's mouth and he ground his crotch against Brendan's— steel on steel.

Brendan stopped struggling in his arms. His tongue eased past Tuck's, snaking into Tuck's mouth while his arm came around Tuck. They kissed for several minutes, feverishly at first, then slowing down to explore, to suckle, to tease. Tuck pulled back, drawing his tongue down Brendan's sandpapery chin and along his throat. He gave in to his impulse to lightly bite the firm, muscular flesh where Brendan's neck met his shoulder.

Brendan was breathing hard. He didn't resist, he didn't push him away. Emboldened, Tuck slid lower, pushing up Brendan's shirt. He ran his hands over Brendan's firm abs and along the warm skin to his chest. Leaning up, he flicked at a nipple with his tongue, savoring how it stiffened to his touch.

He grabbed the second quilt from the end of the bed and drew it over their bodies, completely hiding his own head, hoping this cover would allow Brendan to let him continue.

Blindly he groped for Brendan's fly, pulling open the metal

button at its top and forcing the zipper past the mound of his cock and balls. The underwear was loose—boxer shorts from the feel of them. Eagerly, praying Brendan wouldn't stop him, Tuck reached inside for the prize.

Brendan's cock was hard, the skin taut and hot to the touch. Tuck gripped it, feeling the pulse of a vein throb against his palm. He inhaled the intoxicating scent of Brendan's musk. Brendan was trembling. A part of Tuck knew he should slow down, better gauge Brendan's responses, give him a chance to adjust.

Lust overruled these considerations and he opened his mouth, never in his life so hungry for what he was about to taste. He closed his lips in a wet, tight circle over the head of Brendan's fat cock. A soft moan was audible above the covers.

Emboldened by Brendan's response, Tuck lowered his head, taking the cock fully into his mouth. He moved his hand down to stroke the delicate balls beneath, while suckling the rigid shaft as best he could within the confines of the boxers and the suffocating down quilt covering his head.

After several minutes of greedily feasting, Tuck felt Brendan's hand on the back of his head and inwardly grinned. The gesture subtly changed what was going on between them. No longer merely the shy virgin swept up in the moment by the more experienced and persistent lover, that touch proved Brendan's active desire, his complicity in the act.

Brendan began to shudder, his hips thrusting toward Tuck, forcing his cock deep into Tuck's throat. Brendan's fingers gripped Tuck's hair, twisting it as he stiffened and uttered a small, stifled cry. Brendan's cock was too far back in his throat for Tuck to taste its sweet emission, but he could feel the spurting release pulsing through the shaft.

Brendan loosened his grip and sagged back against the cot.

Tuck drew back, allowing the spent shaft to fall from his lips. He pushed the covers from his head and pulled himself, sweating, up beside Brendan.

He expected to find Brendan limp, eyes closed, even feigning sleep. Instead he found him, raised on one elbow, his eyes wide open and blazing with a kind of inner fire.

"Tuck," he breathed, infusing the word with such passion Tuck found himself blushing.

Brendan took him into his arms. He held him so tight Tuck could barely breathe. After a moment he disengaged himself from the binding embrace and moved back a little to see Brendan's face.

"You okay?"

"Yeah. I have absolutely no fucking idea what the hell just happened, but I think I'll live."

"I didn't exactly mean to do that." Tuck dipped his head apologetically. "It just sort of happened."

"Well, I didn't exactly fight you off." Tuck thought he detected hesitation, even regret in Brendan's voice. Now that Brendan had come, was the hetero voice of reason raising its irrational, homophobic head?

Tuck tried to keep his voice light. "But?"

"Does it make me...?"

Tuck knew what Brendan wanted to say. He took an almost cruel pleasure in refusing to help him along. "What I mean is," Brendan continued, no longer meeting Tuck's eye, "I've never, uh, you know, been with a guy." He dragged a hand over his face and through his hair.

Tuck prompted, "So you're wondering now if you're..."

"Well, yeah, you know. Because I've only ever been with women before and now..."

Tuck couldn't bear the thought of Brendan pulling back, pulling away. All the carefully controlled emotions and desires held in such tight check these past six weeks had burst from the dam of Tuck's reserve. He wouldn't, he couldn't go back to pretending they were just colleagues, just friends.

He leaned up over Brendan, pushing him down onto his back. His still-raging erection made him bold. "Don't think so much. Not now. Just kiss me." He lowered himself over Brendan, letting his full weight pin the smaller man beneath him.

To his vast relief, Brendan didn't resist him. Instead his lips parted to meet Tuck's, his arms coming around him. As they kissed, Tuck couldn't help rubbing against Brendan's crotch. His cock, still trapped in denim and cotton, remained hard as bone. Would he be reduced to the same ignoble release as poor Jamie, coming in his pants like a kid?

To his stunned surprise, he felt Brendan's hands fumbling at his fly. Tuck lifted his hips to allow easier access. When Brendan's fingers brushed the exposed head of his penis, which was sticking out of the top of his bikini briefs, he nearly came then and there.

Too hot to care if Jamie saw, if Brendan was having second thoughts or if an entire rescue crew walked in on them right then, Tuck pushed his jeans and underwear down his thighs. He rolled to his back, his cock levitating over his belly. Silently, desperately, he willed Brendan to touch him again.

Brendan obeyed the silent command, capturing the length of Tuck's shaft and pulling up hard. Tuck groaned. Brendan's hand moved down, pumping Tuck's shaft as he'd pumped his own in the shower. The incredible, perfect friction, the sensual buildup of the last hour and the knowledge it was Brendan touching him, made him come within minutes. Brendan held on as Tuck jerked and shuddered, spurting his seed over his stomach and chest.

He lay waiting to catch his breath, chilled as the sweat that had broken over his body began to evaporate. His pants and underwear were twisted at his knees. His cock was flagging and sticky with ejaculate.

He turned to Brendan with a small laugh, touching a blob of semen. "I'm a mess. I need a shower."

"But we agreed to conserve...?" Brendan made the remark a question.

"Conserve, not forbid altogether." Tuck paused, pretending the idea had just come to him. "Say, what about this? We could shower together. Save water and fuel that way, right?"

As he watched the other man's face close, he could have bitten off his tongue. It was one thing to jerk each other off, both still half-dressed, hidden beneath blankets and the cover of darkness. It was quite another to face one another, naked, the heat of desire for the moment cooled by their recent release.

"I, uh, I think I'll pass," Brendan demurred. "I'm really beat." He turned away.

"Sure, whatever." Tuck rose swiftly from the cot, hitching his jeans into place, using the tail of his shirt to wipe away some of the evidence of his recent passion. Stepping past the still-sleeping Jamie on the floor, he fled to the bathroom.

Jamie lay silent as a stone, his mind whirling. He had awoken to the whispering rustle of the quilts, to ragged breathing and barely audible gasps of pleasure. It took a second for his fogged brain to clear and process what he was hearing.

So he'd been right. There was something between those two. Or at least there was *now*. He wanted to sit up and see just exactly what they were doing. He wanted to get up and join them but didn't dare.

Instead he pulled open his pants, reaching in to stroke his erection. He was both sexually excited by what he was hearing and lonelier than he'd ever felt in his life. *What about me?* He wanted to demand to be included, but he kept his silence, his hard cock wrapped in his hand as Tuck and Brendan took their pleasure without him.

Tuck, who only that afternoon had draped his hard, sexy body over Jamie's, using the massage as an excuse to touch him. Jealousy rose like bile in his throat at the thought of Brendan now possessing the man Jamie wanted for his own.

I had him first.

He pushed away the irrational thought. He'd come like a teenager on Tuck's leg. That didn't mean they were going out. Though Tuck had been gracious about it, he probably thought Jamie was just a kid—not a serious contender for his affections.

He heard them moving, their voices low as they murmured together. He jerked his hand from his jeans and shut his eyes when he heard footsteps approaching. The bathroom door opened and closed. He could hear the sound of running water in the shower.

The image of tall, dark Tuck and the slighter, blond Brendan pressed against each other, naked beneath the spray, filled him with jealousy and lust in equal measure. The unsatisfactory orgasm he'd stolen with Tuck had barely taken the edge off a building desire. It felt good to touch himself.

Closing his eyes, he visualized the two naked men as he stroked. He imagined himself between them, on his knees, taking first one and then the other hard cock into his mouth. He pulled up hard against his shaft, aware he only had a few minutes before the lovebirds emerged from their shower.

The scene shifted. He was on his hands and knees, Tuck behind him, poised to penetrate, Brendan beneath him, Jamie's cock down his throat. Jamie reached into his jeans pocket, finding and retrieving a crumpled tissue. He spit on his hand and returned to his cock, rubbing in a frenzy, his eyes squeezed tight, his breathing labored. He came in several hard, jerking thrusts, aiming the ejaculation as best he could into the tissue.

He heard the scrape of metal against wood and stiffened. It sounded like a cot being moved. *Shit.* Someone was in the room. For a fraction of a second he couldn't fathom who it could be. He would have heard a rescue plane's arrival, wouldn't he? As reason returned, he realized he had just assumed they'd gone into the bathroom together to continue where they'd left off in the bed. Apparently he'd been mistaken.

Stuffing the gooey tissue into his pocket, he zipped his fly and pulled down his shirt. Lifting his head, he peered through the rosy gloom cast by the portable heater.

Brendan was walking from Tuck's cot to his own. He appeared to be fully dressed. As if sensing Jamie's gaze, he turned toward him. It was too dark to see his expression clearly, but by his body language, Jamie had a sense Brendan was uncomfortable. Had he heard Jamie jerking off? His face burned with embarrassment at the probability.

Yet when Brendan spoke, his voice was casual, perhaps elaborately so—it was hard to say. "You're awake."

"Yeah. Just woke up," Jamie lied, fairly certain Brendan had heard him, but damned if he'd admit it. He sat up and a wave of dizziness assailed him. He dragged his hand over his eyes, waiting for it to pass.

Brendan moved closer to him and sat on the edge of an empty cot. "You all right?"

"Yeah, I'm fine. Just sat up too fast."

"You need help getting up?"

Jamie shook his head and rolled himself to his knees. He stood, fighting off the second round of dizziness. He'd had a lot to drink and not much to eat in the last twenty-four hours. Brendan, meanwhile, had returned to his own cot, where he stretched out, still fully clothed, and pulled his blanket to his chin. The silence was heavy. There was so much left unsaid between them. Jamie opened his mouth to try and then shut it again.

He pricked his ears. Something was different. In the stillness he strained his mind, trying to come up with what it was. The shower was no longer running. The night was...*quiet.*

"Oh my God," he burst out. "Listen to that."

"To what?" Brendan leaned up on his elbows.

"That's just it. Nothing. The wind. It's not howling. The building isn't rattling. It's quiet."

Brendan flung the covers aside and leaped up, heading for the window. He pulled back the flap and stared into the gloom. "You're right. The winds have died down, at least for now."

Grabbing his flashlight, he shone it through the glass. Snow was still falling, but it was falling down, instead of sideways. Brendan clicked off the flashlight and turned on the reading lamp beside his cot.

"Not much we can do now. We should probably try to get some sleep. Then in the morning we can see if we can't get a door or window open. I want to find that satellite dish and see if it sustained damage. If we could get it working, we could get contact back with the outside world."

Relief surged through Jamie. Weakly he sank to his own cot, for a moment the distraction of Brendan and Tuck as lovers pushed to the back of his mind. If the storm was over, or nearly so, they would be rescued. Maybe not tomorrow or even the next day, but there was hope. Winter hadn't yet set in. The sun still hovered over the horizon. Soon they would be back in the States, telling their tale to friends over mugs of beer.

Tuck came out of the bathroom in his jeans and undershirt, toweling his hair. "Jamie. You're up. I hope we didn't wake you." A secret look flashed between Tuck and Brendan, slipping like a dagger between Jamie's ribs.

Didn't think of that while you were getting each other off, huh? Jamie pushed aside the thought, focusing on the positive. "Listen to the wind, Tuck. Or rather the lack of it. The storm's over."

"Not necessarily over," Brendan interjected. "Don't get your hopes too high, Jamie. Sometimes there are lulls and then the winds and snow pick up again. But it is a good sign."

Tuck tilted his head, listening. "Hey. That's great. Did you check outside? Can you see anything?" His voice was laced with excitement.

"Still snowing." Brendan's voice was calm. "I thought we could wait until morning. See if we can't dig out and get our satellite signal back."

Tuck moved toward his own cot and sat on the edge. "I guess we should try to get some sleep, huh? Though I, for one, don't know if I'll be able to shut my eyes. I'm too hungry, for one thing. We could feast on oatmeal and energy bars."

"What a great idea." Brendan laughed. "Who could pass up such gourmet fare?"

Nothing, Jamie realized, was going to be said. Nothing was going to be admitted. Whatever had happened between Tuck and him, between Tuck and Brendan, all of it would be swept back under the rug. The storm's end meant an end to whatever sexual exploration might have taken place between them.

Though he knew he should be elated that soon they would

be going home, he felt oddly bereft, aware he had lost something just beyond his grasp, something that had never really been his.

Chapter Six

"I still think we should try to get out there and see about the dish." Brendan took a sip of the strong coffee Jamie had brewed, which he'd tried to make palatable with powdered creamer. It was hugely disappointing to realize the wind had picked up again. He quietly doubted the blizzard was over, but at least they would be able to check the satellite connection.

He glanced at Tuck and was disconcerted to discover Tuck was watching him with a small, enigmatic smile. Looking quickly away, Brendan felt his face heat. He was thirty-four years old, for crying out loud, and didn't know how to act. Tuck, so handsome with those dark, brooding eyes and large, strong hands. Tuck, who had driven him nearly insane with pleasure. Tuck, whose own cock had been like granite beneath Brendan's trembling touch.

What the hell had happened last night? Was it only a physical release, the kind of thing that happened in the trenches during war or between prisoners on death row? Was he just so lonely, horny and drunk that even another guy had seemed better than nothing?

He was skirting the real questions, and he knew it. Tuck was not just another guy. He was the one person who had somehow penetrated Brendan's reserve, slipping past the carefully constructed walls that kept the world at a proper distance.

Did one encounter with a guy make a person gay? Was he ruined now for women? Did he care? Brendan was a scientist. He liked things neatly defined and properly ordered. He derived deep satisfaction from taking the chaos in the world around him and breaking its codes, plundering its secrets, rendering it tame. How in the hell was he supposed to figure this one out? What hypotheses should he pose, what experiments should he conduct?

And what of Jamie? How much had he overheard when he was supposedly sleeping off his vodka binge? Had Jamie witnessed their teenaged fumbling beneath the covers? He'd certainly been awake enough in the moments after Tuck went into the shower.

Brendan had heard Jamie's sudden, labored breathing and had thought at first he was in the throes of a bad dream. When the breathing became a pant, followed by the telltale gasp of a climax, Brendan had been both put off and aroused as it dawned on him what he was hearing.

Based on Jamie's startled reaction, and his lie that he'd just woken, Brendan was pretty sure Jamie hadn't realized he was in the room. Which must mean he had believed Brendan and Tuck were together in the bathroom. There were two separate shower stalls, so Jamie wouldn't have necessarily assumed they were showering together. So what if he did? He was openly gay—how could he object?

Jamie finished his oatmeal, drank some coffee and looked expectantly at Brendan. For one horrible second, Brendan thought he was going to say something about last night. He nearly sagged with relief when Jamie stood, his tone all business. "Let's do this thing."

They had decided not to try opening the windows in the

sleeping quarters, so as not to lose the heat there. Because of the wind patterns, while huge piles of snow had drifted along parts of the building, there were spots swept clear.

They pulled on their boots and parkas and left the warmth of the kitchen to see what door or window might be most accessible. Each of the three labs had several windows along the outer walls to take advantage of the warming greenhouse effect of the sunlight, and there were exit doors at both ends of the hallway, as well as one that opened onto the shed in which the diesel generators were kept.

Carrying flashlights, they made their way down the frigidly cold hallway to the generator shed to turn on the second generator that powered the lab area. Tuck advanced into the room and moved toward the diesel engines. He flicked the switch. Brendan expected to hear the dull roar of the engine coming to life, but nothing happened.

Tuck knelt in front of the machine, shining his flashlight over the control panel. "Huh. That's strange. It's completely dead. No power." He turned back to Brendan and Jamie. "While I'm figuring out what's wrong, we could divert power from the other generator to the labs so you can see your way out."

Brendan nodded his approval. Tuck moved to the second generator and opened the control panel. Consulting a small manual that sat atop the generator, he punched in a series of codes. All at once the hallway outside the door was lit by electric light. Tuck turned back with a triumphant smile.

"Now you can see what you're doing. Meanwhile I'll see if I can't figure out what's wrong with this one."

"Sounds like a plan." Brendan patted the walkie-talkie strapped to his belt, the twin of which was on Tuck's belt. "We'll head down to the wet lab. I think that's our best shot for finding an accessible window. If we get the window cleared, we'll just head outside and check conditions. Signal if you need anything."

Tuck nodded. "You do the same."

Brendan and Jamie made their way to the wet lab. They had agreed in advance Tuck would remain inside, walkie-talkie at the ready in case they encountered obstacles or needed his assistance. Brendan carried a shovel and additional outer gear. Jamie had a small, portable snow blower slung over one shoulder.

Two of the thick thermal panes of glass were completely blocked by snow, but the third one was mostly clear. The dawn cast a pearly gray light over the snow-covered surface that stretched as far as the eye could see. Though the gale force winds had abated, snow continued to whirl and eddy in a frenzied dance.

They pulled on their gear. Brendan unlocked the window and pushed the panel outward. A fierce gust of icy wind hurled snow into the room. Each man pulled his scarf up over his nose and mouth. Jamie leaned out the window and turned on the snow blower, clearing away the top few feet of snow before jumping down.

Brendan followed, sinking up to his thighs in the deep snow. Though the sun was obscured by the cloud cover, the glare was still blinding against the whitewash of snow and ice. After pushing the window closed as best he could, he lowered his goggles and began to shovel behind Jamie.

Even dressed as he was, in long johns, a thermal long-sleeved vest, two pairs of thick socks, moleskin pants, a fleece jacket, an insulated headband, a neck scarf, a pair of gloves covered by a pair of insulated mittens, and double-boots with a thick, insulated sole and his hooded parka, he could feel the cold.

It was hard to believe only the week before they'd been playing football, comfortable in only a few layers of clothing. Then the weather had been calm and sunny. Now the icy wind blew needles of freezing snow in their faces.

Making slow progress, they eventually found their way to the side of the building where the satellite dish was housed. It was set up on a communication tower, most of which was covered in a snowdrift. Even from where they stood, Brendan could see the dish was bent at an odd angle, no longer lined up properly to receive satellite transmissions.

Being smaller and lighter, he climbed the ladder on the tower, with Jamie remaining below to spot him. The physical energy expended to move through and clear the snow had Brendan's heart pounding, and though his clothing was designed to whisk perspiration from his skin, sweat trickled down his sides.

He reached the top of the tower and, leaning against it, pulled off his mittens and stuffed them in his pockets. He worked quickly, aware of the danger of frostbite, despite the lined leather gloves. He repositioned the satellite to its designated coordinates as best he could. The dish itself didn't look damaged, as far as he could tell. He was eager to get back to the shelter to see if they were back online.

The wind was picking up, and conversation was nearly impossible. He had to yell to make himself heard. "I repositioned the dish. Let's hope that does it."

Jamie nodded, watching as Brendan put on his mittens. The wind was blowing so hard now they were pushed partially sidewise as they trudged and shoveled their way through the piled snow. Jamie again led the way, the small snow blower chugging furiously, spewing a thick stream of snow as they went.

***

Tuck tinkered with the broken generator in an effort to determine the cause. He had opened the door of the control panel and was going through several of the trouble-shooting diagnostics, so far to no avail.

His head had begun to hurt and he was feeling sick to his stomach. *Probably a hangover. We drank like fish last night.* Promising himself some aspirin and a large glass of water once he got the generator going, Tuck tried to focus on his work.

Even while concentrating on his task, a constant play of memories scrolled through his head—the look of fire in Brendan's eyes when he'd said Tuck's name with such raw emotion, Jamie's embarrassed expression when he realized he'd come in his jeans, the taste of Brendan's cock, the scent of Jamie's desire.

None of them had said a word this morning, himself included. There had been many furtive glances and rapid looking away. It would have been almost funny if it hadn't mattered so much. He could hardly bear the thought of leaving Brendan now, of them each returning to their lives, separated by distance and by their inability or unwillingness to explore their feelings.

As crazy as it was, a part of him regretted that the blizzard had died down and they would soon be rescued. What an ideal opportunity for the three of them to explore whatever was happening between them.

Wait a minute—the three of them? Take Brendan and himself first. Though he knew one twenty-minute groping session didn't mean they were in love, there was definitely something going on, and it went beyond mere lust.

With Jamie the picture was less sure, but the attraction was definitely there as well. As spontaneous as it had been, the heat between them was real. Tuck's cock rose at the memory of their kiss. Jamie, at least, didn't have the hang-ups and hetero angst Brendan was dealing with. He'd made his desire for Tuck very clear.

What would Jamie think of a three-way? Brendan, after all, was very easy on the eyes. What hot-blooded young gay guy could resist?

Tuck shook his head. He felt dizzy and his thoughts were becoming fuzzy. He tried to focus on the manual and the control panel, punching the sequence indicated to check the ventilation system. The word, "Danger—High Levels of Carbon Monoxide Detected" flashed across the screen.

That would explain his sudden distinctly unpleasant symptoms. Tuck stood on unsteady legs, thinking to check the ventilation ducts. All at once his knees buckled and the bright blue-painted metal of the generator rose at an alarming speed to meet his face.

Brendan pushed the button on his walkie-talkie—two short and one long beep to indicate they were heading back. Holding the walkie-talkie to his ear, he waited for the answering confirmation beeps, but heard nothing. A faint sense of unease passed through him. Why wasn't Tuck responding?

Maybe he was so engrossed in repairing the generator he hadn't heard it, or maybe he hadn't heard the return signal over the noise of the generator engine. Well, they'd be back in soon enough and then they could check in. They'd already been outside for nearly half an hour. It took another fifteen to work their way back around the building to the unlocked window.

Jamie helped Brendan climb through first, making a stepping stool with his hands. Brendan then turned to take the blower and shovel Jamie handed through the window and reached out his hand to pull Jamie inside. Though both of them were at peak physical strength and used to the altitude and cold, they lay slumped on the floor for several minutes until their hearts slowed and their breathing steadied.

Jamie was the first to get up. He took off the ice-and-snow-encrusted parka and pulled off his boots. "Man, I don't like that wind. Was it my imagination or was it getting worse the longer we were out there?"

"I'm afraid it was. I don't think we're out of this thing yet. But at least there was enough of a lull to check the satellite. Hopefully now the communications network will be back online." Brendan didn't add his fear that if the winds kept up, the dish would probably fail again. No point in jinxing things.

Jamie looked relieved. "Let's go see how Tuck's doing with that generator. Then I want some hot tea."

Brendan hoisted himself to his feet and pulled off his frozen outer gear. Together they made their way out of the lab and down the hall to find Tuck.

"Brendan! Hurry!" Jamie stood frozen just inside the door of the generator shed. Horror poured over him as he stared transfixed at the bloody scene before him.

Tuck was slumped on the ground beside the generator, his face resting in a pool of bright red blood.

"Oh, my God." Brendan pushed past Jamie and knelt beside Tuck. Carefully he rolled him to his back. "It's his forehead. It looks like he hit his head somehow." Brendan bent over him, his ear close to Tuck's mouth. He grabbed Tuck's wrist between two fingers and waited.

"He's breathing and his pulse is steady, thank God."

Jamie came to kneel beside Brendan. Pulling the scarf from around his neck, he wiped at the blood still trickling over Tuck's face.

"Go get the first-aid kit," Brendan barked roughly. "Run."

Jamie ran across the hallway to the closest lab. There was a first-aid kit in every lab, as well as one in the living quarters. He could hear Brendan calling Tuck's name, shaking and trying to rouse him. In a moment Jamie returned, opening the white plastic container and removing antiseptic, gauze and bandages.

Tuck remained unconscious. Brendan and Jamie worked to staunch the blood flow, cleaning the wound and applying the bandages. "It's stuffy in here," Brendan noted. "I'm feeling kind of dizzy myself."

"Yeah. And I'm getting a headache." Their eyes met and understanding clicked in both of them at the same instant.

"Check the ventilation ducts." Brendan jabbed a finger toward the ceiling. "And let's get him out of here."

Jamie, using a small stepladder, climbed up to the vent and found it was completely blocked by snow, which would explain the carbon monoxide buildup from the enclosed generators. Tuck must have fainted and hit his head on the engine on the way down.

"Give me something. That broom." He pointed and Brendan obliged, handing it to him. Using the handle, Jamie pushed out as much snow as he could and climbed down. "The fans are working again. That should clear the air some."

Brendan tried once more to rouse Tuck, but he remained limp, his eyes closed. Brendan's lips were pressed into a hard, straight line, his brow furrowed. Jamie had the uncomfortable feeling he was trying not to cry. Not that he blamed him. He felt like crying himself at the thought of Tuck lying unconscious in a pool of blood while they sat resting in the lab before coming to find him.

Carefully they lifted him between them, Jamie carrying his body, Brendan his legs. As fast as they could, they took him down the hall and back into the warmth of the living quarters.

After passing through the kitchen, they settled him onto his cot. While Brendan removed Tuck's jacket and gloves, Jamie undid Tuck's boots and pulled them from his feet.

"Shit." Jamie looked up at Brendan's epithet. "He's bleeding again."

Jamie knelt beside Brendan. A red circle of blood had seeped through the gauze and surgical tape covering the wound. Using two fingers, Jamie applied pressure to the wound, silently willing it to stop bleeding.

"Tuck." Brendan shook his shoulder. "Wake up. Come on, man. Wake up."

To their relief, Tuck stirred and opened his eyes. His gaze was unfocused until it lighted on Brendan's face. "Brendan." He smiled and Brendan returned the smile. Jamie flinched inwardly at the piercing barb of jealousy ripping through his guts. They only had eyes for each other. He didn't stand a chance.

He forced his feelings aside. "How do you feel, Tuck? You took quite a fall. Can you remember what happened?"

Tuck turned his gaze from Brendan's face and looked at Jamie. He squinted, his expression confused.

"Do you know who I am, Tuck?"

"Sure. You're Jamie." He bestowed a smile just as warm as the one he'd given Brendan, and despite his trepidation that

Tuck had suffered a concussion, Jamie's heart softened with longing.

"We think you were poisoned by a CO buildup in the shed. The ventilation ducts were blocked."

"That's right." Tuck tried to sit up. He sank back, the color draining from his face.

"Take it easy." Brendan's voice was ripe with concern.

Tuck continued, "There was a high CO reading on the screen when I ran one of the diagnostics. I still didn't get the generator running though. I must have passed out." He felt the gauze covering the still-bleeding wound.

"You took quite a fall, looks like, and must have hit your head on a sharp corner on the way down." Brendan touched his shoulder. "We found you unconscious when we got back from the expedition."

"What happened out there? Was the dish intact?"

"It had been blown from its coordinate position. I set it in place, so we'll have to see. We haven't had a chance to check yet if we're back online."

"Man, I'm really sorry about this. I should have recognized the symptoms sooner. I thought I just had a hangover." He grinned weakly. "Jesus," he whispered, his skin pale and waxy. "I don't feel so good."

"I'm sorry we didn't find you sooner." Brendan stroked Tuck's hair. "You need stitches to close that wound. I'm pretty handy with a needle. Let's get you sewn up and get that bleeding stopped once and for all."

Jamie stood and turned away, annoyed by the lovey-dovey tone of Brendan's voice. "We've got oxygen too, in the clean lab. It wouldn't hurt to get some pure oxygen into your bloodstream to counteract the carbon monoxide. That's what's making you feel like crap." He left the room in search of the oxygen tank and facemask.

When he returned, Brendan was in the process of injecting an anesthetic at the site of the wound. Tuck winced as the needle slipped below the skin, his face still very pale. Brendan had removed the bloody bandage, revealing a gash about an inch long on Tuck's forehead.

"Let me know if it hurts. That injection should numb you up pretty good." In addition to fitness and stamina training, as well as altitude training, Jamie had also taken an extensive first-aid course in preparation for this assignment. Still, he was relieved Brendan had stepped forward with confidence for this particular job. Stitching moleskin in a classroom setting was a far cry from the real thing.

Brendan pulled on surgical gloves and prepared the needle and thread. Jamie watched, fascinated and a little sick at the sight of the needle being drawn through Tuck's skin. Tuck's eyes were closed but he didn't seem to be in any pain from the sharp needle, thank goodness. Brendan worked carefully, producing small even stitches. When he was done, he tied a knot and snipped off the thread. After applying an antiseptic ointment, he put a fresh bandage over the wound.

Jamie moved forward, securing the facemask over Tuck's nose and mouth. "This should ease the nausea and the headache as it counteracts the CO. Let me know when you're feeling better."

He knelt beside the bed, monitoring Tuck as Brendan moved about, putting away the first-aid supplies. Brendan returned. "Here. Have some water."

Gratefully Jamie took the glass. He hadn't realized he was parched until that moment. He drank deeply, finishing the glass. Brendan took it and went back into the kitchen, returning with a fresh glass.

Tuck stirred and opened his eyes. "I'm feeling better, I think." His voice was muffled beneath the facemask. Jamie released the straps, careful not to touch the bandage.

Brendan nudged Jamie aside, his focus on Tuck. "You should rehydrate." He cradled Tuck's head, holding it as Tuck sipped. Jamie turned away.

Chapter Seven

"I wonder how long he was out before we got to him." Jamie lay sprawled across the couch, a cup of tea rapidly cooling in his mug.

Brendan sat at the card table, his laptop in front of him. He looked up sharply at the question. "What's that supposed to mean?"

Jamie was startled by the vehemence in Brendan's tone. He felt himself getting defensive. "It *means* we were sitting around on our asses catching our breath after we climbed back through the window, while Tuck was lying there unconscious in a pool of his own blood."

Tuck was sleeping, his forehead swathed in bandages. The horrifying memory of him lying crumpled and bleeding in the generator shed lingered in Jamie's mind, and he suppressed a shudder.

"You're right." Brendan's tone became conciliatory. "I'm sorry I snapped. I was just sitting here feeling guilty about Tuck. I should have paid more attention when he didn't immediately respond to my all-clear signal."

"You mean with the walkie-talkies? You signaled when we were done and heading back, right?"

"Yeah, and he didn't answer. I just figured he was distracted with whatever he was doing. In retrospect, though, he could have already been unconscious at that point. My failure to react could have killed him."

Brendan looked so stricken Jamie opened his mouth to assure Brendan it wasn't his fault. Then the image of Brendan pushing him away so he could hold Tuck's head, lifting the glass of water to his lips like a lover, reared itself in his mind. His generous impulse dried up like water vapor in the dry Antarctic air.

He knew he wasn't being fair. Brendan had taken good care of Tuck, far better than Jamie could have done on his own. Calling on his better nature, Jamie attempted some reassurance. "He was pretty lucid after regaining consciousness so the odds are the blow wasn't too severe. You did a great job on the stitches, by the way. Maybe you missed your calling."

"Wait until it heals and he sees the scar that's left before deciding." Brendan snorted and tossed his head. He glanced at his laptop screen, his eyes widening.

"What? What is it?"

"It's *working*. I reinstalled the communication software to see if I could get the satellite connection running again and we've got Internet. We're connected again. Oh, thank *God*."

Jamie leaped from the sofa and hurried over to see. He watched as Brendan scrolled through the main email account. He saw over a dozen emails, many marked *urgent*, from headquarters at the National Science Foundation.

Tears of relief sprang to his eyes. Now that the worst of the storm seemed to have passed and communication was restored, surely it was only a matter of hours before they were rescued.

Brendan turned to him, excitement raw in his voice. "Get my cell phone, will you? It's next to my cot. See if we have service."

Jamie retrieved the phone and flipped it open. As if on cue,

79

it began to ring. "Hello? This is Jamie Hunter at the West Antarctic Lab." There was static on the line. "Can you hear me?"

After a pause and some clicking sounds, a deep voice boomed over the line. "Hello. We can hear you. Thank goodness you're back online. We've all been worried sick about you. How is everything?"

He recognized the voice of Hank Shafer, one of the senior primary investigators on the project. Jamie was grinning so hard his cheeks hurt. Brendan had jumped from his chair and stood close by, bouncing on the balls of his feet. Jamie half expected him to grab the phone. He turned away, too eager for a voice from the outside world to relinquish the phone just yet.

"We're okay. Tuck took a fall while repairing one of the generators but nothing life threatening. We managed to get outside this morning for the first time and reposition the satellite dish. It had been blown off its coordinates by the high winds. When can you get us out of here?"

Jamie tried not to interpret the long pause that followed as ominous. His palms were sweating, making the small phone slippery in his grip. His heart tapped painfully against his sternum.

"Is Brendan there, Jamie?"

Wordlessly, Jamie held out the phone to Brendan, trying not to sink under the weight of foreboding settling over him. "Aaronson, here." Brendan's dark blond eyebrows formed a V, his mouth turning down at the corners.

"Right. No. We hadn't had a chance to check the weather forecasts yet. We only just managed to reconnect when you called." Another pause while Brendan listened, his eyes on the floor, his free hand clenching into a fist.

Fuck, Jamie thought. *Whatever they're saying, it's not good.* Anxiously he watched Brendan's face, trying desperately not to leap to conclusions. Brendan wasn't saying much, merely grunting and nodding. Finally he made his goodbyes and hung up.

He turned to Jamie with a shrug. "There's another storm right behind this one. They're predicting it will hit by midafternoon. There's no way they can risk sending a plane or helicopter into it. We're going to have to sit tight another day or two. Maybe longer."

Jamie nodded, swallowing his disappointment like the bitter pill it was. *Are we going to die here?* He squelched the question before it even had a chance to fully form in his mind.

Instead he focused on his frustration. Here he was twenty-five years old, but all he felt like doing at the moment was demanding with a stamp of his feet that Brendan *make* those bastards come get them. *Now.* He was dismayed to realize hot tears had sprung unwelcome into his eyes. He needed to get away from Brendan's pitying look, but where the hell could he go?

Remembering the blood in the generator shed, he spoke without looking at Brendan, not wanting him to see the tears of disappointment and fear. "I'm going to clean that mess out in the shed. Tuck doesn't need to see that when we go back out to work on the generator."

"Good idea. Be mindful it might still be toxic in there. Only stay as long as you need." Brendan walked back to the table and picked up one of the walkie-talkie units. He handed it to Jamie. "Put this on and signal me, okay? I'll stay with Tuck."

Jamie kept his face impassive. He pressed the talk button on the unit, causing the other unit, which sat on the table, to beep. Satisfied, he hooked it onto his belt. Taking a mop and bucket from the kitchen supply closet, he added water and bleach to the bucket. He further armed himself with a roll of paper towels and some strong disinfectant spray.

Putting on his parka and a pair of gloves, he left the warmth of their living quarters and ventured down the frigid hallway toward the shed. The working generator's engine rumbled, the sound echoing against the bare walls of the room. The ventilator fans were whirring, a good sign the room was probably safe for breathing once again.

Nevertheless, Jamie was determined to get in and out as quickly as he could. He drew in his breath as he stared at the bright red blood splattered and smeared over the floor. It seemed too red to be real, obscene against the pale gray linoleum.

Poor Tuck. Jamie's heart contracted with pity at the thought of him lying there alone. Setting down his bucket, he went to work cleaning the mess. His mind wandered back to Brendan's words.

I'll stay with Tuck.

"Yeah, I bet you will," he muttered aloud. Life was so fucking unfair. He'd probably die here, stranded with two gorgeous guys, watching from the sidelines while the two of them made secret love in the dark, spurred on by their mingled lust and desperation...

Jamie was distracted from his fanciful, dark thoughts by the beep of the walkie-talkie at his belt. He depressed the button. "Yeah?"

"Just checking. You okay in there?"

"I'm fine, thanks. Nearly done." When Jamie finished, a pale pink stain remained on the light green linoleum, but at least it looked a good deal better than it had before. With a last look around the shed, he pulled the door shut and walked back to the living quarters, the bucket of pink water sloshing at his side.

He returned to find Tuck propped against his pillows, Brendan seated close beside him. Tuck was spooning soup from a mug. Jamie stifled a strong urge to race to his side and fling his arms around him.

"You're looking much better," he said instead. "How's your head?"

"It's okay, actually, thanks." He smiled, warming Jamie to his toes. "There's some pain where Dr. Aaronson stitched me up but the mean ol' doc won't give me any pain meds." He grinned at Brendan, who smiled back and patted his arm.

"You know we can't risk that with the possibility of a concussion. That's all we need, to have you slip into a coma on our watch, right, Jamie?"

Surprised to be included in the equation he thought only equaled two, Jamie forgot for a second to be jealous. "Yeah. Not on our watch."

Tuck handed the mug to Brendan and settled back against his pillows. "I'm so tired. I think I'll just take a little nap." He closed his eyes, his dark lashes brushing his still-pale cheeks, and crossed his arms over his chest.

Jesus, was Tuck worse than he'd thought? Was there trauma to his brain? He hadn't seemed disoriented or confused, but he certainly was sleepy. Brendan hadn't moved from his seat by the bed. Did he plan to keep vigil for the rest of the day?

Jamie moved closer and sat on the edge of the cot. He touched Tuck's shoulder, wishing he could lie beside him. A spasm of pain washed over Tuck's face, though he didn't open his eyes.

"Don't touch him," Brendan barked. "You're bothering him."

Stung, Jamie stood abruptly and turned away. Who died and elected Brendan head of the fucking world? He walked over to the sofa and slumped down on it. He just wanted to get out, to get away.

What if they never did? What if the winter winds had come early, and the snow and ice sealed them in like a tomb for the duration?

He'd barely begun to live. He'd never even been in love. Not the kind of heart-stopping, gut-wrenching love he'd read about and dreamed about and yearned for. Was this how it was going to end? With him watching while Brendan nursed Tuck back to health, so they could go have furtive sex beneath the covers while he drank himself into a coma?

He dropped his head into his hands. Tears wet his face and seeped through his fingers. *Fuck.* He did not want to cry, and certainly not in front of stoic, calm Brendan. But he was tired— exhausted. And scared. He took a breath and hiccupped, a sob escaping from his lips.

He felt rather than saw Brendan sit beside him. Brendan dropped a heavy, comforting arm over Jamie's shoulders. He held himself stiff, jerking away from the offered embrace without removing his head from his hands. This unexpected tenderness was going to be his undoing. He refused to give Brendan the satisfaction of seeing him cry.

The arm around him tightened and despite himself, Jamie leaned into it. He was so lonely, so frightened, so tired of keeping up the brave front. A second arm came around him, pulling him toward the other man. "Hey, shh, it's okay, Jamie. It's okay. It's all going to be okay."

Brendan's voice stripped his last defenses and Jamie began to cry in earnest. He buried his head against Brendan's chest and sobbed, great, gulping sobs. He cried as he hadn't since he was a child, his shoulders shaking, barely able to catch his breath through the gasping sobs that rose from deep inside.

Brendan held him tight, rocking him gently. Jamie kept his head hidden in the folds of Brendan's flannel shirt, comforted by the soothing motion even as he cried.

Eventually he quieted, resting his wet cheek against the warmth of Brendan's chest, lulled by the slow, steady beat of Brendan's heart. He wished he could just stay there until the rescue plane arrived.

But no, soon Brendan would realize he'd stopped crying. His altruistic impulse to comfort Jamie would be overwhelmed by his realization he was hugging a guy, or at least the wrong guy, and he would pull away. Why put off the inevitable?

Jamie pulled back, expecting Brendan to loosen his embrace. To his surprise, Brendan held him tight, if anything tighter than the moment before. Confused but grateful, Jamie remained as he was, wrapped in Brendan's strong arms. Tentatively, he brought his own arms around Brendan's waist as he nestled against his chest.

He was getting a hard-on. Jesus, Brendan was going to feel his erection and freak out. Jamie dropped his arms and again pulled back, and this time Brendan let him go.

They locked eyes and Jamie couldn't look away. Brendan's pupils were dilated, deep black orbs rimmed with clear gray green glass. He brushed Jamie's wet cheek with his fingers. Without thinking, Jamie put his hand over Brendan's.

Neither moved for several seconds. Jamie became aware of the ticking of the wall clock. They stared at one another, their hearts keeping time—tick, tock, tick, tock...

Brendan was leaning forward, his eyes closing, his lips parting. *He wants me to kiss him.* Jamie shook his head. This couldn't be happening. And yet it was. Jamie didn't move, frozen with indecision and confusion.

Brendan looked so hot, with his blond hair flopping over

his forehead and the sexy three-day stubble over his firm jaw. His lips were lush and inviting, but surely Jamie was misreading his cues? If Brendan was in the midst of discovering his bi side, he was doing it with Tuck, right?

Brendan's eyes opened and he pulled his hand from beneath Jamie's. Still neither spoke. Jamie's lips tingled with lost opportunity and he was suddenly desperate for that missed kiss. He leaned forward, parting his own lips and closing his eyes, praying Brendan still wanted him, that it hadn't been a moment's fluke, already regretted.

He felt the lightest brush of skin on skin, Brendan's lips touching his. He moved a fraction forward, just enough to acknowledge the press of flesh without frightening Brendan away.

Again they remained still, statues caught in a chaste kiss, though Jamie felt like anything but stone. Hot blood rushed through his veins, making his cock throb. Of the two men, Tuck had always seemed so much more accessible on every level. Jamie never would have dreamed of approaching Brendan like this, nor would he have in normal circumstances.

But these were hardly normal circumstances. Even if this was just Brendan reacting off his own fear at their situation, and his own unrequited lusts, who was Jamie to stand in his way? He dared to place a hand on the back of Brendan's neck to pull him closer.

Brendan didn't resist him. Instead his lips parted and Jamie darted his tongue past them, his heart slamming. He felt more like fifteen than twenty-five, certain at any second Brendan would pull away with outrage and disgust.

But Brendan didn't pull away. His tongue touched Jamie's, sending tremors of desire through Jamie's body. Emboldened, he brought his other arm around Brendan and leaned back, pulling Brendan on top of him.

Brendan seemed willing enough. His mouth remained locked on Jamie's as he allowed himself to be dragged forward. Jamie could feel Brendan's erection against his hip. This was no fluke. Brendan was turned on too.

Jamie didn't dare act on this knowledge. For now it was enough just to feel Brendan's strong, hard body over his and taste the sweetness of his kiss. Brendan's cock felt like a steel pole. Unable to resist, Jamie moved beneath him until steel met iron. What he wouldn't have given to feel Brendan's hand on him at that moment, slipping past the waist of his jeans to clutch his aching, throbbing shaft.

He prayed he wouldn't come in his pants, as he had with Tuck. With this thought in mind, he shifted beneath Brendan to get away from Brendan's erection, but the friction only made him harder.

Brendan lifted his head, withdrawing his warm velvet tongue from Jamie's mouth. Jamie opened his eyes, waiting for Brendan to come to his senses and pull away in horror.

He didn't move from on top of Jamie, however. Instead, he leaned down and whispered raggedly, "I don't know what I'm doing."

There was such an appeal in his voice, as if Jamie would enlighten him. Jamie didn't know what the hell he was doing either, but he knew it felt good. He knew it felt better than anything had over the past two days, save for the few minutes with Tuck, which had been stolen bits of heaven.

Whatever was happening, it was better than focusing on the thick sheet of ice on which this building sat, buffeted by snow that was again whipping in a rising howl of wind just beyond these walls. It was better than remembering Brendan's true object of desire lay asleep a few feet away. It was better than being alone.

"You don't have to know," he offered in a whisper. "Sometimes it's okay not to know."

Brendan nodded and dipped his head. They kissed again. Jamie could feel Brendan's heart beating hard and fast against him. He slipped his hands beneath the layers of Brendan's clothing until he touched the smooth, warm skin of his back.

If he could have one wish right then, it would be that their clothing disappear. He longed to feel skin on skin. He hungered to taste a hard, hot cock. He ached to bury his nose in another man's armpit, to lick his nipples, to tongue his ass, to feel the thick invasion of a shaft penetrating him...

Brendan shared at least one of his thoughts, because he lifted himself from Jamie to sit beside him. He unbuttoned and tossed his flannel outer shirt to the floor. In one swift movement, he pulled his thermal undershirt off, revealing a thickly muscled bare chest with a smattering of dark blond curls in a V at the sternum.

Jamie eyed him greedily as he sat and pulled off his own shirt. Everyone on the project was in good shape—it was one of the criteria for working in such a taxing environment at high altitudes—but Brendan was seriously built, his shoulders broad, his pecs pronounced, his abs like a wooden washboard.

What was happening? What the hell did Brendan want or expect? How far did Jamie dare go? His cock was nearly bursting from his jeans, pressing so hard against his fly it hurt. Yet he didn't dare open his pants. Not unless or until Brendan made another move.

Brendan stiffened suddenly, his cheeks suffusing with blood like someone had slapped him. Startled, Jamie followed Brendan's gaze to the sleeping Tuck. Only Tuck wasn't sleeping. He was raised on one elbow, a sardonic grin on his face.

"So, was I going to get an invitation, or is this just a party for two?"

Chapter Eight

"Tuck, you're awake." Brendan stood, his mind clicking back on as the blood rushed from his cock to his face. Jesus, what the hell had been going on? First Jamie was crying, sobbing against his chest like a child, then they were kissing. *Kissing?*

He looked from Tuck to Jamie, who, like himself, was shirtless, a thin gold chain flat against his smooth chest. Though his eyes were still red from crying, Jamie smiled and shrugged, as if to say, *What now?*

Brendan grabbed his outer shirt and pulled it on, hastily buttoning it. When he got to the bottom he realized he'd mismatched the buttons with their holes. He felt like an idiot with both Tuck and Jamie now regarding him with bemused expressions.

What was he supposed to say? What was the protocol between three *guys*? Whatever he'd shared with Tuck the night before, did that make them lovers? Had he breached some unstated but understood agreement with Tuck by kissing Jamie?

Most important, beneath all these questions was the main one. What the hell was happening to him? The world felt as if it were tilting on its axis. He no longer knew who, or what, he was.

Jamie reached for his undershirt, which he pulled over his head. He shook his light brown hair from his eyes, though it promptly fell forward again. Tuck sat up and swung his legs over the side of his cot. He swayed slightly and lay back down, passing his hand over his face.

Brendan moved toward him, forgetting his own tortured confusion. "Dizzy? You probably just sat up too fast." He knelt by the cot. "Listen." He spoke in an undertone. "There was nothing really going on just now. Or if there was, it doesn't mean... That is..." He faltered, embarrassed. "I don't even know what the fuck I'm trying to say."

Tuck reached for him, pulling his head down to the mattress. "You don't owe me any explanation." He stroked Brendan's hair, his touch soothing. Brendan closed his eyes, for once just giving in without resisting either himself or what was happening. He felt suddenly drained.

"Jamie." Tuck's voice floated over Brendan's head. "Come here."

Jamie. Brendan was struck with remorse. As soon as Tuck woke, Brendan had all but forgotten the younger man. Was he going to spend the rest of their time together feeling guilty and responsible for everyone?

He hadn't meant to kiss Jamie. It had just happened. He couldn't deny how hot it had made him. But when Tuck had spoken, it was as if Jamie had disappeared. He only had ears and eyes for Tuck. Was he in love? Or just lust, a lust ignited by their fevered groping the night before?

Tuck continued to stroke Brendan's hair. His touch was soothing and Brendan relaxed some. Tuck said, "I still feel a little woozy. Why don't you push another cot over here and we can all three lie down? I think we've got some things to talk through, don't you?"

His eyes still closed, he heard rather than saw Jamie beside him. "Good idea," Jamie agreed.

Brendan lifted his head and pushed himself to his feet. Why not? Usually the one in charge, no matter the situation, for once he felt completely out of his ken. He'd let the other two run the show for a while.

He helped Jamie to push the nearby cot toward Tuck's. They spread their quilts over the adjoining wooden frames. Tuck scooted toward the middle and patted the side by the wall. "Jamie, you lie here."

Brendan lay on Tuck's other side. He was silently grateful Tuck had positioned himself between them. He didn't want to be in the middle, not on any level, or so he told himself.

Once the three of them were reasonably well settled, Tuck asked, "So were you able to reestablish communication?"

Brendan told him about the phone call. Tuck nodded soberly without reply. They lay quietly for a while, listening to the wind, which had resumed hurling snow against the walls of the building, making siege.

"We've still got plenty of water, right?" Tuck asked.

"Yeah." Brendan nodded, forcing away his sudden desire for a cold glass of Coke. "Enough water and energy bars to last a month."

"And enough booze too," Jamie volunteered with a laugh.

"Excellent point." Tuck grinned. "So it seems to me we should look at this as an opportunity. We were all set to hightail it out of here two days ago. Odds are we each would have gone our separate ways. Now we're, well, for want of a better term, stuck here together.

"We have no new research to do, nothing and no one to distract us. We've all spent the last six weeks working really hard. Maybe we can look at these few days as a bonus vacation for all our hard work."

A fleeting smile gave way to a sober expression. "I've been lying here thinking about it. I could have died back there in the generator shed. Another twenty or thirty minutes breathing that carbon monoxide and I would have been history. And you guys—you could have been literally blown away out there, covered in drifts of snow, suffocated and frozen to death before I could find you—if I could find you."

Brendan shuddered at this macabre scenario, though he knew Tuck was right. Tuck continued. "There's a slim chance they won't be able to get through before winter. There's a chance we'll have to spend the next four or five months here, subsisting on whatever they can airdrop down to us."

Jamie made a small gasping sound. Tuck turned to him and put his hand on Jamie's arm. "I don't think it'll come to that. I really don't. In a day or two, three at the most, we'll be out of here. They're going to do whatever they can. They'll be watching the weather patterns like hawks and send in their best pilots, you can count on it.

"But my point is, this is *it*. For right now, this is all we have. We are truly being forced to live in the moment. It makes you think." He paused, staring up at the ceiling so intently Brendan thought there might actually be something up there. He looked too, but saw only the dark blue insulated fabric surrounding fluorescent light fixtures.

"Really, we're just a microcosm of the human condition. Whether we're here a day, a month, a year, fifty years—our time on this earth is finite." This time he turned to Brendan. "Life isn't a dress rehearsal, as they say. This is our chance to discover things we might have only dreamed of before." His voice dropped to a caress, his dark eyes locked on Brendan.

"So, forgive me for being so blunt, but where do I fit in all this?" Jamie leaned up on one elbow, facing the others. "I mean, I saw you two last night going at it." Now it was Brendan's turn to gasp. He looked away, wishing he could disappear.

"Oh, you did, huh? Why didn't you join in?" Tuck's voice was light, but Brendan noticed the slight flush on his cheeks.

"Didn't think I was invited," Jamie quipped. He, too, kept his voice light, but Brendan could hear the hurt in his tone. It occurred to him Jamie might have strong feelings for Tuck. Something had definitely been going on between them when he'd walked in on them, and while Tuck might have claimed, and even believed, they'd just been fondling—his word—to Jamie it might have meant a great deal more.

"Seriously." Tuck's voice was gentle. "That's why I want to talk now. Bring everything out into the open between us. Don't forget, I just now woke up to see you two with no shirts on, and those weren't pistols in your pants. I kind of doubt you were thinking about doing laundry."

Jamie started to say something but Tuck stopped him. "No, hear me out. I'm not accusing. It's not my place and not my intention. I'm just saying, right now things are tense enough for us without adding to it by keeping secrets from each other. Okay?"

Jamie nodded. "Okay. We'll do a *real* truth or dare. Except no dare, just the truth."

"Exactly." Tuck sat up, touched the bandage on his forehead and lay back down.

"Take it easy." Brendan was glad to have something to focus on. All this talk about truth was making him decidedly nervous. "Before we do anything else, we should have a look at that wound. Make sure it's not still bleeding. I've never done stitches on a real live person before."

"You haven't?" Jamie sounded surprised. "You sure seemed to know what you were doing."

Brendan shrugged. "It's not rocket science. Or even geophysics." Jamie and Tuck laughed. Brendan arose and returned a moment later with the first-aid kit. Tuck moved toward the edge of the cot and Jamie brought a chair over from the card table.

Carefully Brendan peeled back the surgical tape that held the gauze in place. An inch of dark brown stitches crisscrossed Tuck's forehead above his right eye like a centipede. The site was swollen and red but there was no seepage Brendan could see and the wound looked clean. He squirted some antibiotic ointment over the stitches and applied some fresh gauze and tape.

Jamie, meanwhile, brought over several energy bars, a jug of water and a bottle of Southern Comfort. "We missed lunch. We can have a picnic right here so Tuck doesn't have to sit up too much. I've got mocha, chocolate, oatmeal and peanut butter. Any takers?"

"I'm not sure Tuck should have any alcohol." Brendan watched as Jamie twisted the cap on the one-hundred-proof liquor and poured a few jiggers' worth into each glass.

"It's okay, doc." Tuck grinned. "I promise not to drive."

He wasn't acting like someone with a concussion, so Brendan decided not to make it an issue. It was strange to feel so protective of someone. He wasn't used to it. Deciding he was thinking too much, he drank the strong, sweet liquor in one burning gulp and held out his glass to Jamie for a refill.

"Hey, slow down. We've got all night." Tuck accepted the glass from Jamie and sipped at his, his eyes playing over Brendan.

Jamie, too, threw back his first shot and poured himself

another. Tuck was leaning against a mound of pillows. Jamie and Brendan sat cross-legged on either side of him.

They munched on the dense, chewy energy bars, drank water and sipped at their drinks, no one saying much for a while. Tuck ate two bars. Brendan was pleased to see he had an appetite. He himself didn't seem to have much of one, but he forced himself to finish a bar and drink plenty of water.

Tuck pulled two pillows from behind his head and placed them on either side of him. He patted the pillows, indicating Jamie and Brendan should again lie down beside him. "Now, where were we?"

"We were talking about secrets," Jamie offered. Brendan felt a twinge of anxiety but said nothing. Maybe if he were very quiet they wouldn't notice him. He grinned to himself, feeling like the youngest one there.

"Yeah." Tuck turned to Brendan. "Secrets." He turned to meet Tuck's steady gaze. "Brendan, I don't think it's a secret anymore how I feel about you. Being stranded here, getting hurt." He touched his forehead. "It's really made me face up to the fact that this is it. I don't want to spend another year pining for you and wondering what if...I need to know. This time I'm not letting you go without finding out."

Brendan shook his head, puzzled on one level, aware on another, for hadn't he done the same thing? But he wanted to hear Tuck say it aloud, and so he prompted, "Another year?"

"Since last summer. I told you already. I can't believe it was entirely coincidence we ended up on another assignment. It's fate. We were meant to be together, if not for a lifetime, at least to discover what there was or is between us."

The Southern Comfort was doing its job. Brendan's normal reticence was decidedly easing. If they wanted secrets, he would spill one of his own. "If you want to know the truth—no secrets—it wasn't entirely a coincidence."

"What do you mean?"

"Think back. How did you first find out about the project?"

"I got a letter asking if I was interested."

"From?"

"From Dr. Winston, at NSF."

Brendan took another fortifying gulp of the Southern Comfort. "Take a guess who my thesis advisor at Stanford was." He watched the dawning realization on Tuck's face and he nodded, unable to suppress a chuckle. "That's right. Dr. Theodore Winston, Science Chair at Stanford and Director for Geosciences at the National Science Foundation. He also happens to be on the board of the Kramer Institute."

Tuck leaned back heavily against the pillows, a dazed look on his face. "So you mean...you wanted to see me as much as I..."

Brendan felt his face heat, but he held his ground, for once not looking away. He nodded.

Tuck tilted his head. "But the few emails we exchanged— you were so reserved. I figured you were just drunk that night and, once sober, ashamed of whatever you thought had gone on between us."

Brendan didn't deny this. He had pulled away, scared not of Tuck, but of his own reactions. "Not ashamed. Confused. And...scared. It's scary to realize you're attracted to a guy. At least for me it was—is."

"Hey, guys." They both looked at Jamie. "Is this just about the two of you, or is there room for me?" Jamie's tone was teasing but Brendan's heart lurched toward him, connecting with the loneliness beneath his words. He understood that loneliness, probably better than Tuck, who always seemed to be the center of things, easygoing and everybody's friend, at home with both men and women, comfortable in his own skin.

Tuck turned toward Jamie and stroked his face. The simple gesture of intimacy made Brendan catch his breath. Without realizing it, he found he was touching his own cheek.

"There is room for you, Jamie. Lots of room. This is our chance, the *three* of us. After what happened between you and me yesterday, we can't deny our mutual attraction. And then there's you and Brendan. Since we're not keeping secrets, you guys have to admit there was definitely something afoot between you when I woke up from my nap."

Jamie turned from Tuck to Brendan, who somehow managed to hold the gaze. "Is that right, Brendan?" Jamie's voice held challenge, but also yearning. "Is there something between us? Are we all three in this together?"

Tuck turned to him as well. Brendan looked from dark eyes to blue and swallowed, nearly overwhelmed with emotion. "Yes," he managed to whisper.

The storm had begun again in earnest, raging and rattling around them, highlighting both the desperateness of their situation and the warmth and coziness of their shelter. He wasn't going to hide from his feelings—not anymore. Tuck was right. This was all they had—all anybody had. It was time to start living—honestly and without fear of rejection or loss. For the first time in his life, there was literally no place left to hide. For the first time, he realized he didn't want to.

Tuck listened to the sound of running water, marveling at the turn of events. If he hadn't fallen and hit his head, would this even be happening? He touched his bandage. The wound throbbed dully beneath it, the numbness of the Novocain having mostly worn off.

Oddly, he didn't mind the pain. Or, more accurately, he felt so keenly alive and so grateful for that life, the pain was simply a testament to it. Having brushed death, however briefly, he felt this life was all the sweeter, even if they were stranded on the edge of the world.

He thought about the two very sexy men now showering, each no doubt in a separate stall. Jamie was definitely ready to play. Though by far the youngest of the three, Jamie was surely the most sexually experienced, at least where guys were concerned. He imagined Jamie would teach the two of them a thing or two. His cock tingled at the thought and he slipped his hand into his jeans, idly stroking it.

Brendan's reaction was uncertain, but based on their brief but very hot tryst of the night before, he was also ready and willing to learn. The thing was to keep Brendan feeling comfortable. Not to rush the action and make him retreat back to the safety of his definition of himself as straight.

How did a person get to his mid-thirties without ever connecting to a side of himself that was obviously there? Brendan didn't suddenly turn bi when Tuck kissed him. The feelings were there. They were there the year before, and no doubt had always been there, dormant and ignored.

He guessed he shouldn't really be surprised. Most guys ignored their feelings, and not just their sexual ones. Society certainly didn't encourage men to connect, especially with homosexual desires. In fact, they were soundly discouraged. Maybe the real wonder was how many guys did actually find the courage and honesty to explore their true natures, even in the face of discrimination and rejection.

Jamie was the first to emerge from the bathroom, toweling his wet hair. "Did you conserve water by showering together?"

"What do you think? We've got ourselves a live one, Tuck. A virgin." Jamie shook his head. "Ironic, isn't it? He's the oldest, the head of the team, a natural leader, but now things are kind of turned on their heads."

"Yeah. It's good to keep that in mind too. We want to help him explore, but not scare him to death in the process."

Jamie moved toward the footlocker at the end of his bed. He dropped his towel to pull on his underwear. Tuck noticed for the first time the small tattoo of a snake curling around Jamie's left hip, its red, rippling tongue pointing toward his ass.

As Jamie pulled on a pair of jeans, Tuck realized he didn't want him to add a shirt. He wanted to admire that sexy physique, to run his hands over the skin and the muscles beneath, to taste the flesh and flick the nipples with his tongue.

He sat and swung his legs over his cot, pleased there was no accompanying wave of dizziness. "Let's turn on both space heaters. Make it warmer in here so we don't need all these damn layers."

He stood carefully, still experiencing no ill effects. He retrieved the second space heater and turned it on, watching a moment as the oil-heated filaments turned from silver to red.

"You don't think we should conserve in case...?" Jamie didn't finish the sentence.

"Nah. Not tonight. Let's make tonight perfect. For all we know, it's our only chance." This was true. The winds might die down sufficiently that they'd be rescued the next day. How strange to realize he no longer wanted that. At least not yet. There was too much at stake here. Too much he wanted first.

He unbuttoned his flannel shirt and pulled it off. Jamie, still bare-chested, watched him with unabashed desire, the bulge at his crotch rapidly rising. Tuck pulled his thermal shirt over his head and moved closer to the space heater.

Jamie approached him, his blue eyes flashing. "I want you, Tuck. You said no secrets. I have to know. Be honest with me—trust me, I can take it. Am I just thrown into this mix as an afterthought? Or do you want me too?"

Tuck moved closer, so they were standing face-to-face, only inches apart. He put his hand on Jamie's hip and pushed at the waist of the jeans so they slid lower, revealing the snake tattoo.

He drew his thumb over the ink, a bright green diamond pattern outlined in black, the whole thing no larger than a man's finger. It seemed almost alive, twisting and undulating along the curve of his hipbone.

He looked up from the tattoo into Jamie's eyes, while he drew his palm along Jamie's skin from his hip to his flat belly. The jeans hung loose and he slipped his hand into the front of Jamie's pants and beneath the elastic of his underwear.

Jamie's cock was erect. Tuck curled his fingers around it and gripped him hard. "I want you too. Don't doubt it for a second." He kissed him on the mouth and then stepped back, letting him go.

Jamie leaned forward, rubbing his erect cock through his jeans. "You can't just do that to a guy and then stop." His eyes were narrowed with lust.

"Only for the moment, Jamie. I don't want to start something with you, only to have Brendan come out again and freak out, you know?"

Jamie dropped his hand to his side. "Yeah, you're right. We have enough real-life drama with this storm without adding any more of our own."

Tuck nodded, relieved Jamie understood. "Now, let's go see what's taking Brendan so long."

"Yeah. If he's wasting water, we might have to spank him."

Tuck grinned back at him. "Hey, remember, we don't want to totally freak the guy out."

Jamie winked broadly and licked his lips. "Not right away, anyway."

Chapter Nine

Brendan stepped out of the bathroom just as they turned to enter. He was fully dressed, not that this surprised Jamie. Brendan smiled and ran his fingers through his hair, which was dark gold when wet.

Jamie hooked his thumbs into his back pockets, aware this dragged his jeans down enough to reveal most of the snake tattoo. He stared at Brendan, daring him to notice. Brendan's gaze swept over both men's bare chests and he caught his lower lip in his teeth.

"We wondered if you were ever coming out." Tuck's voice was teasing. "Looks like you're all dressed up and no place to go." Tuck sidled closer to Brendan and tugged at the top button of his outer shirt. "We turned on both heaters. You won't need all these layers."

Brendan stood stiffly, allowing Tuck to unbutton his shirt and push it from his shoulders. If Tuck was aware of Brendan's discomfiture, he gave no sign. "Let's watch a movie. We can use your laptop."

They walked into the sleeping quarters. Having something to do seemed to ease Brendan's anxiety. He went to the laptop and flipped open the lid. "I should check the weather too." He sat down and began to type. His brow furrowed and he frowned. "Fuck." His voice was quiet, but Jamie heard the anguish in it and glanced up sharply.

Brendan looked from him to Tuck with a pained expression. "We lost it again. The satellite connection." They were all silent. What was there to say? Jamie took a deep breath and exhaled. He was done panicking over the situation.

When he'd cried—something he hadn't done in years—it had somehow cleansed him, not only of his sorrows, but of his fears. Whatever was going to happen, he wouldn't change it one iota by flipping out. What Tuck said was true—this was all they had. Today, this moment, this life—this was it. No dress rehearsal, no do overs.

He looked from blond, sexy Brendan to dark, handsome Tuck and smiled, surprised that his calm wasn't forced. He shrugged. "We know they're monitoring the situation. They aren't going to forget about us. It's not like they could get through now anyway. We might as well relax and enjoy the time we have together, right?"

Tuck's expression eased, the worried pucker between his eyebrows smoothing. "You're right, Jamie. Where's that Southern Comfort, anyway? It's kind of growing on me." He turned to Brendan. "What DVDs do we have that we haven't already watched six hundred times?"

"Steve had the big collection." Brendan paused, pursing his lips. "I actually have a few old movies you might like." He moved toward his cot and opened his footlocker, rummaging through piles of rumpled clothing. He held up a DVD case. "How about this? A classic."

"What is it?" Tuck asked.

"*Lawrence of Arabia.*"

Tuck raised his eyebrows. "With Peter O'Toole?"

"Yep."

"That's a great movie. I heard he's gay."

Jamie, not familiar with the movie and barely aware of who Peter O'Toole was, perked up. "Who, Lawrence of Arabia or Peter O'Toole?"

Tuck laughed. "Both, actually." Jamie found himself more interested in the movie.

Brendan popped the DVD into the laptop and turned it toward the sofa, their usual spot for watching movies. Tuck touched his bandage and made a face. "I think I should probably lie down, don't you? Why don't we set up the laptop so we can see it from my cot? We can keep this double bed setup."

"Yes, of course. I'm sorry. I wasn't thinking." Brendan shifted the card table so it was facing the cots, while Tuck winked at Jamie, who grinned. The situation was funny in a way—the two of them plotting to seduce the straight guy, everyone tiptoeing around what they knew was going to happen.

Jamie still held himself back. He wasn't going to push himself between those two, but he wouldn't be a jerk either, playing hard to get. He'd just go with the flow and see where it took him. He busied himself with pouring portions of the sweet, strong liquor into the juice glasses. Tuck, meanwhile, rearranged the pillows so they were resting against the wall.

The three of them settled in, leaning back against the pillows, their drinks in hand. By unspoken agreement, Jamie and Tuck lay on either side of Brendan. They watched the movie awhile, sipping their drinks. After their second round, they set their glasses aside and focused on the film, which so far, to Jamie's surprise, was pretty good for something made forty-five years before.

"Hey," Jamie observed. "That O'Toole guy actually looks like you, Brendan."

"You think so?" Brendan shrugged.

"He does look like you." Tuck turned from the screen to examine Brendan's features. "It's your wavy hair. And also the sensual mouth and the strong jaw line." He ran a finger along Brendan's jaw. Jamie watched, fascinated, as Brendan actually shivered to Tuck's touch.

Jamie scooted closer so his leg was touching Brendan's. He dared to drop his hand to Brendan's thigh. Brendan turned toward him, his gaze moving from Jamie's hand to his face. Tuck's hand appeared on Brendan's other thigh. Brendan's head whipped in his direction.

Tuck's voice was soothing. "Relax, Bren. We aren't going to eat you. We just want to touch you. To explore a little. That's okay, isn't it? We all agree we want this, right?"

"Yeah." Brendan's voice was soft. He allowed Tuck to push at his shoulder until he was lying flat between them. On the screen, Lawrence appeared over the top of a huge simmering sand dune, his white robe whipping in the wind, but Jamie stopped even pretending to pay attention.

He slid down beside Brendan, moving his hand along Brendan's thigh to his crotch. Boldly, he cupped the inviting bulge, delighted to feel it harden beneath his fingers. He met Tuck's eye and they smiled complicity. However nervous Brendan was, he wanted this.

Tuck tugged at the hem of Brendan's undershirt. Jamie took the other side and together they pulled it upward. "We need to even the playing field," Tuck asserted when Brendan offered a very mild protest. He lifted himself enough to allow them to remove the shirt.

"Nice." Tuck ran his hand over Brendan's curling blond chest hair. Brendan closed his eyes, his cheeks turning pink. Tuck grinned over him at Jamie. Jamie moved his hand from Brendan's jeans to his broad chest. He licked his finger and used it to circle a nipple. The nubbin stiffened and rose at his touch. He did the same to the second nipple.

"Hot," Tuck whispered. He was leaning over Brendan so his face nearly touched Jamie's. All at once they turned to one another over Brendan's body, their lips meeting. Jamie's cock responded like an inflating balloon, lengthening and engorging, catching uncomfortably in his underwear. He wanted to take off his jeans but didn't quite dare. Not yet. He did open his fly, reaching in his underwear to free his bent cock.

Tuck drew back from the kiss, his eyes fixed on Jamie's crotch. Jamie removed his hand. The elastic from the waistband of his underwear was cutting into his skin, just below the head of his swollen cock, which was hidden in the shadow of his open jeans.

Brendan lay inert beneath them. Tuck glanced at Brendan's face and Jamie followed suit. Brendan was watching them, his eyes hooded, his lips parted. Jamie stroked Brendan's chest, resting his hand over Brendan's heart, which was thumping rapidly beneath his fingers.

Tuck unbuttoned Brendan's fly. Jamie grasped the metal tag of the zipper and dragged it over the bulge straining at Brendan's crotch. He noted with some amusement Brendan's baggy boxer shorts, and resisted the temptation to reach inside the open fly.

"Hey." Brendan lifted his head, his hand moving to cover his crotch.

"Hey, nothing." Tuck pushed his hand away. "It's good, Brendan. Remember, it's all good. We're not doing anything we don't all three want."

"Yeah," Jamie echoed.

He watched with mingled lust and jealousy as Tuck lowered his head until his mouth was on Brendan's. Brendan's chest was heaving but he didn't push Tuck away. Jamie's gaze traveled down Brendan's body to his open jeans.

He had to swallow to keep from choking on the saliva that rushed to his mouth at the thought of taking Brendan's hard cock down his throat. What had the two of them been up to last night? How far had their fumbling beneath the covers gone? Would Brendan let him suck him off?

There was only one way to find out.

While the other two kissed, he tugged at Brendan's jeans, managing to push them aside enough for access to the fly of Brendan's shorts. He placed his hand over the blue cotton that was all that now stood between him and Brendan's cock and balls. Brendan made a muffled protest, his hand again moving to cover his crotch.

Jamie watched with wry amusement when Tuck blocked the apparently anticipated action. He kept his own hand in place, enjoying the heat and throb of Brendan's erect cock beneath the thin fabric.

While the two men kissed, Jamie's cock strained in its confines. Emboldened by his lust and the sexy scene before him, Jamie slipped off the bed long enough to pull off his jeans and underwear.

Despite the best efforts of their heating system, the room still wasn't warm enough to prevent the shudder of cold that undulated through his body. He realized for the last half hour or so he hadn't even noticed the howling wind, which now cut through his consciousness like a knife. Forcing himself to ignore it, he turned his attentions back to Brendan's erection, which beckoned like a Siren.

He crouched naked on the bed at Brendan's side. Reaching into the boxers, he wrapped his hand around the erect shaft. Pulling it through the fly, he squeezed the head between thumb and forefinger and lowered his mouth to lick away the drop of pre-come his action produced.

So sweet, so inviting—it had been far too long since Jamie had tasted cock. Hungry for it—starving would be a better word—he lowered his head, taking the shaft as far as the constrictions of Brendan's clothing would permit. Brendan groaned and Jamie was vaguely aware Tuck had pulled back from their kiss.

Tuck's hands were suddenly in his way and Jamie raised his head, mildly annoyed to be interrupted. Then he realized what Tuck was doing. He was pulling Brendan's boxers down his narrow hips. The shy, virginal Brendan, to Jamie's pleased amusement, lifted his ass to help out. Jamie helped too, dragging the pants down Brendan's legs. Between them, they had him naked in a moment.

Eager to return to his task, Jamie lowered his head again, sucking the length of Brendan's long, hard cock deep into his throat. He wasn't interested in teasing Brendan, in making it last, in running his tongue under and around the shaft until he made him cry with sexual frustration.

No, this was about Jamie. Hungry, horny, needy Jamie. He gripped Brendan's balls, eliciting another groan.

"Jesus, that's hot, Jamie." Tuck's voice was husky. "Do you like it, Brendan? Do you like what Jamie's doing to you?"

"Mmph," came Brendan's inarticulate reply. Jamie grinned against Brendan's cock and slipped a hand down below the balls. He ran his fingertip in a light circle around Brendan's asshole, his own cock tingling at the thought of plunging himself into it.

He glanced upward. Tuck was draped over Brendan, his mouth covering one nipple, his hands moving over Brendan's bare torso. Brendan's breath was ragged, a series of syncopated gasps, his hips thrusting up to meet Jamie's kiss. Jamie slipped his other hand beneath Brendan. Cupping each cheek, he gripped Brendan's ass to hold him in place.

Bobbing like a piston, he reveled in the hot, smooth steel of Brendan's shaft, purposely choking himself on it until his nose rested against Brendan's pubic bone. As he suckled the cock with his throat muscles, Brendan's gasps shifted to a long, drawn-out moan. He tensed, the globes of his ass tightening in Jamie's cupped grip.

Jamie felt powerful. He felt alive. Brendan and Tuck might be older and certainly professionally more accomplished, but they had nothing on him when it came to sucking cock.

With a cry, Brendan released his seed. Greedily Jamie swallowed the bittersweet jism, milking Brendan's cock until his rigid muscles eased and Brendan sagged limply against the mattress. He held the shaft in his mouth another several seconds before letting it go.

Satisfied, he knelt back on his heels, his own erect cock jutting proudly from his belly. Brendan's eyes were closed, the skin over his cheeks, throat and chest flushed from the orgasm.

Tuck's dark eyes were burning. At some point he too had pulled off his jeans and was as naked as the others. Jamie's gaze traveled down Tuck's long, hard body, stopping at the erect, thick cock pointing toward his in invitation.

"Jesus, Jamie. That was something to watch. I guess you've done that a few times before, huh?"

Jamie laughed and wiped his mouth with the back of his hand. "A few times, yeah."

He looked toward Brendan, who had opened his eyes. "Jamie." His deep voice was throaty. "That was *incredible.*"

"Now, wait a minute." Tuck put his hands on his hips, the gesture made silly by his erect, bobbing shaft. "What about me?

You're not saying he did a better job, are you?"

Brendan looked stricken and began to blush, the color darkening his cheeks from orgasmic pink to brick red. Jamie quickly realized the extent, or rather twofold nature of his embarrassment.

By asking the question, Tuck was admitting outright in front of Jamie that they'd had sex the night before, something Brendan had apparently been trying to conceal. In addition, he was being put on the spot, forced to compare lovers and, by definition, find one of them wanting.

Jamie knew Tuck was only teasing, and he waited with some amusement to see how Brendan would get himself out of this one. "What? I, uh, no. I didn't mean that. That is, you were great too..."

Tuck began to laugh and Jamie joined him. Brendan glared from one to the other for a several seconds before a smile curled over his face and he too began to laugh. He lunged toward Tuck, catching him in a playful hold, pulling the taller man down in his strong grip.

They tussled, each grappling for a superior position. Jamie's laughter died as his cock hardened at the sexy scene. He grabbed his shaft, stroking the length of it. His balls ached and he still hungered for them both.

As the two men played at wrestling, Jamie could feel the dynamic subtly changing between them. The tussle shifted more to caressing and touching each other's bodies. Jamie wondered how or if he should join them, aching to become a part of the sexy romp, but hesitant without an express invitation.

Tuck chose that instant to look at Jamie, who still knelt on the edge of the bed, his cock loosely held in his hand. "Hey, you. Come down here. We need you. We want you." He held out his free arm, the other being trapped beneath Brendan's naked body.

Jamie didn't react right away, wondering if Tuck thought he spoke for both himself and Brendan. Then Brendan held out his hand. "Yes. Please."

Their faces were open, smiling, the invitation sincere. It was as if someone had lifted a mantle of loneliness from his shoulders he hadn't even known he'd been wearing. Jamie felt lighter in spirit than he had in weeks. He leaned down and the two men parted, making a space for him in the middle and wrapping him tightly in their arms.

"So, what's that tattoo about? You have some kind of snake fetish? Are you a member of a secret cult that uses snake venom as an aphrodisiac?" Tuck traced the green and black snake with his finger, stopping at the flickering red tongue. Jamie was on his back between them, his cock a thick, hard rod resting against his flat stomach.

Jamie snorted and shook his head. "Nothing so exciting. Actually there's a name under there. The name of the guy who I, at the ripe old age of twenty-one, *thought* I was in love with and would be *forever*. We had our names tattooed on each other's hips. We thought it was romantic. Then we broke up six months later and I ended up with a snake. I just picked it at random, to cover the name. No deep significance."

"I like it." Brendan, who was lying on his side facing the other two, drew his finger in turn along the snake's body. "That must have hurt, huh? Needle on the bone like that."

"Yeah. It hurt like hell both times, but the guy was pretty quick."

Tuck let his hand wander over Jamie's stomach to his smooth, broad chest. Brendan was moving his hand down

Jamie's thigh, the fingers sliding inward toward his crotch.

Jamie closed his eyes with a contented sigh. His cock was thick, long and straight. If they'd been alone, Tuck wouldn't have hesitated to take the beautiful member into his hands and mouth, but he was still cautious about Brendan.

He looked to him now, studying his face. Brendan was eyeing Jamie's shaft. Tuck imagined he saw both lust and uncertainty in his eyes. Brendan, perhaps aware of Tuck's gaze, turned to him. "I still can't quite believe this is happening."

Jamie, his eyes still closed, offered in a deadpan voice, "It's not, Brendan. You're just dreaming. You'll wake up later and still be straight as an arrow, don't worry."

"Jamie." Tuck laughed and shook his head. Jamie wasn't going to give poor Brendan any slack, that much was obvious. It occurred to him Jamie might be jealous. He was an observant guy and he wasn't blind. He had to know there was a special attraction between Brendan and himself.

Which didn't take away from the very real desire he felt for Jamie. The guy was seriously appealing. It had been so hot it almost hurt to watch him deep-throating Brendan with such phenomenal skill and obvious pleasure. Tuck's cock twitched at the memory. He wouldn't mind burying his cock in Jamie's tight little ass. Would Jamie like that? Was he a bottom or a top or both? How about Brendan?

Slow down, he reminded himself. Things were already moving at an incredibly fast pace, especially for a guy who defined himself as straight until only the day before. Maybe he'd just *show* Brendan how it was done. Let him watch from the sidelines for a while, no pressure.

He leaned over and tongued Jamie's nipple. It rose against his tongue and he bit down, hard enough to make Jamie suck in his breath. He sat up and gripped Jamie's shaft, letting his eyes meet Brendan's.

Brendan's eyes were hooded, his expression intense. He seemed frozen in place, watching, waiting. Tuck hoped Brendan understood this about all three of them—there was no need for possessiveness or jealousy. His gaze still on Brendan, Tuck massaged Jamie's cock.

"Yeah. Oh, yeah." Jamie approved, apparently. Tuck pulled up, lifting the shaft until it was perpendicular to Jamie's body. With his other hand, he cupped Jamie's balls, heavy and hot in his grip.

Tuck noted Brendan's cock had risen, its tip touching Jamie's thigh. He turned his attentions back to Jamie, taking his second nipple between his teeth, enjoying the rush of power when Jamie again drew in his breath. His cock hardened in Tuck's grip.

So he liked a little erotic pain, did he? Tuck bit harder and Jamie moaned. "Yes," he whispered, in answer to Tuck's unspoken question. Tuck bit the other nipple, his hand moving faster over the granite-hard shaft.

Jamie began to squirm and shudder, gripping and twisting the bed sheets between his fingers. "God. So good. Yeah." His words were interspersed between sighs of pleasure and gasps each time Tuck bit down on a pert nipple. When he sensed Jamie was about to come, he dropped his hand abruptly.

Jamie opened his eyes, lifting his head. "Hey," he protested. "Why'd ya stop? Don't stop. So close."

By way of answer, Tuck dipped his head, his mouth open in an O. He closed his lips over the crown of Jamie's cock, creating suction. "Oh," Jamie moaned, his head falling back to the pillows. Tuck lowered his head farther, his tongue tickling a path down the underside of the shaft. He didn't stop until he had impaled himself to the hilt.

"Jesus," Jamie murmured fervently. He put his hand on Tuck's head, his fingers wrapping in Tuck's hair. Tuck was crouched on his knees over Jamie. He bobbed up and down the slick shaft, his own cock aching. Grabbing it, he pumped himself, moaning against Jamie's cock.

He wanted Brendan behind him. He wanted Brendan to take his hips and position his cock at Tuck's ass and fuck his brains out while he sucked Jamie to orgasm. Of course that didn't happen. Shy Brendan remained where he was, his eyes glued to the scene.

Tuck let go of the unlikely fantasy and focused his full attention on pleasing Jamie. He liked Jamie's scent—beneath a clean soap smell was his own spicy essence which reminded Tuck of cloves and incense.

He lifted his head, replacing his mouth with his hand. His hand was large enough to cover most of the shaft in his grip. Without letting go, he shifted on the bed, scooting between Jamie's legs. "Draw your feet up," he ordered. "Heels touching your ass."

Jamie obeyed. Tuck saw that Brendan had wrapped his hand around his erect shaft and was moving it up and down as he gaped at the scene before him.

Tuck returned his focus to Jamie. He let Jamie's rigid shaft go while he focused on his balls, licking in a circle around each one. He sucked one into his mouth, tonguing the delicate sac and then letting it go, only to capture the other one. He nudged it lightly with his teeth, eliciting another of those sweet, sudden gasps.

Jamie's fingers again found his hair, pulling and twisting as he writhed beneath Tuck's touch. *I wonder if he could come just from me licking and nibbling his balls.* Jamie was shuddering and groaning. Surprised at such an intense reaction, Tuck glanced upward and understanding dawned.

Brendan was holding Jamie's cock, his fingers curled around the shaft. He was leaning over, his mouth near but not touching the cock, his hand pumping it slow and hard.

Tuck's cock felt like it was going to explode. To distract himself, he returned his attentions to Jamie's balls, licking down beneath them, following the small, ridged line on his perineum that led to the tiny puckered hole below.

He tongued Jamie's ass, drawing a long, guttural moan from his lips. He forced the tip of his tongue past the tight circle of muscle and Jamie, his cock still caught in Brendan's grip, began to buck.

"Oh God, oh God, oh God..." Jamie's voice rose in a crescendo of crashing pleasure. Tuck lifted his head in time to see gobs of spurting semen flying upward, splattering Jamie's belly and chest. Brendan pumped him until the last drops trickled over his fingers.

On an impulse, Tuck grabbed Brendan's hand and licked the pearly ejaculate from his fingers. Brendan pushed his fingers farther into Tuck's mouth. Tuck sucked at them greedily, taking them like a cock into his throat.

"Come lie down, you two." Jamie's voice had the languorous quality of sexual satisfaction. Brendan pulled his fingers from Tuck's mouth. They both turned to Jamie, who lay sprawled, his cock still semi-erect against a nest of brown pubic curls.

Tuck grabbed the corner of the sheet and used it to wipe away the semen from Jamie's stomach and chest. There was even a blob on his chin. "Not bad," Tuck teased.

Jamie smiled lazily. "What about you? You got something there that looks like it's in serious need of attention. Would you concur, Dr. Aaronson?"

"Yeah." Brendan's voice came out hoarse and he cleared his throat. Tuck lay down beside Jamie, his cock rigid, his balls aching. Brendan was watching him, still perched beside Jamie on his knees. His tongue appeared between his lips when Tuck, his eyes on Brendan's face, began to stroke his own shaft.

"Come on." Jamie's voice was soft, entreating. "Join us."

Chapter Ten

Brendan stared at them, letting the surreal moment wash over him. Was this really happening? Not just one man, but two, and him right in the thick of it. He was more sexually excited than he'd ever been with a woman. Was it only because it was taboo? Or had he somehow lived a life that was a lie, his true nature hidden beneath expectations imposed by himself and others?

He knew he didn't want whatever was happening to stop. Maybe it was the crazy situation in which they found themselves, maybe it was the alcohol—he had no earthly idea. All he knew was he wanted these two men and what they offered more than he'd ever wanted anything in his life.

Tuck lay easily beside Jamie, both of them supremely comfortable in their nudity, certain of their physical beauty, which couldn't be denied. Tuck's cock was thick and long. He held it loosely in his big hand, the invitation in his eyes unmistakable.

Brendan looked down at himself, at his cock pointing eagerly toward Tuck and Jamie. Athletic all his life, he was used to being in locker rooms, used to seeing other guys naked, but not like this. Not with erections that wouldn't quit and lust so hot between them the air fairly shimmered with it.

He wanted to touch Tuck's cock again, to feel its hardness

beneath his fingers. He wished the room were dark. He wished Jamie wasn't there watching. He didn't want to make a fool of himself in front of the obviously very experienced younger man. Yet he couldn't deny the fierce desire he felt.

What was happening to him? He enjoyed sex with women, the tight, velvet clasp of a pussy, the soft feel of female skin against his. But he'd never experienced this raging, heart-stopping lust. It was held in check only by his shyness, by the fact it was so new and, until now, not something he would have ever dared entertain, much less act on.

Jamie turned away, reaching for something on the floor beside the cot. He came up holding the bottle of Southern Comfort. After unscrewing the cap, Jamie took a long swig. He held it out to Brendan, his eyebrows raised.

Brendan reached for the bottle and drank several burning gulps. It slithered like liquid heat to his stomach and though it warmed him, he was still frozen where he knelt. He imagined himself scooting forward and crouching between Tuck's legs, as Tuck had done to Jamie, but he couldn't move. He didn't have the nerve.

Jamie turned to Tuck and murmured something inaudible in his ear. Tuck nodded and sat up. "Good idea." He scooted toward the end of the bed and stood, touching his hand to the bandages covering the stitches over his eye.

Guilt assailed Brendan at Tuck's action. Here he was, focused solely on sex when Tuck might be in pain. "You okay? Is it bleeding?" He, too, stood, actually forgetting they were all naked.

"I'm fine. Relax." Tuck held out his hands and smiled. "We just thought we might make things a little easier on you. You look a little anxious." He came around the bed and sat down, patting the mattress beside him. "Sit next to me."

Brendan sat and Tuck sidled close to him. He took Brendan's hand in his and placed it over his erection. Brendan could feel the blood surging in his cheeks, but it was no match for the blood engorging his cock.

He dared to squeeze the shaft, thrilling when it hardened beneath his trembling fingers. Tuck closed his eyes and rested his head on Brendan's shoulder, his cock jutting against Brendan's hand like a kitten demanding to be petted.

Jamie came to sit on Tuck's other side. "That's it." His voice was encouraging. "That's what he needs, Brendan. Just touch it the way you like to be touched."

Brendan moved his hand up and down the rigid pole while Jamie reached beneath him to cup Tuck's balls.

Tuck sighed heavily and leaned back against Jamie's other arm, which was draped over his shoulders.

Brendan looked down at Tuck's cock as he pumped it. He wanted to taste it. To lick it. To see what it felt like to have it in his mouth. Did he have the nerve with Jamie sitting right there? Jamie, who had just given him probably the best orgasm of his life. Jamie, who knew he was a complete novice when it came to men.

As if reading his mind and sensing his hesitation, Jamie lifted his hand from Tuck's balls and rested it lightly over Brendan's. "It's okay. We're all friends here. More than friends. Nobody's judging you. This is your chance, here on the edge of the world, to try what you never dreamed of doing before. Get on the floor on your knees. It's easier that way. Kneel between his feet and have a lick of the best damn lollipop you've ever tasted."

Tuck laughed. "Never had my cock compared to a lollipop before, but Jamie's right. If you don't lick this sucker, I'm going to explode." He squeezed Brendan's thigh. "Please," he whispered. "I need you."

Those three words gave him the final push. Brendan slipped from the cot to the floor and knelt in front of Tuck. His heart was beating too fast and he felt dizzy with nerves, anticipation and lust. Closing his eyes, he gingerly lowered his open mouth over the head of Tuck's cock.

He licked over the slit and ran his tongue experimentally around the rim of the crown. The skin was soft, softer than he would have imagined, silky beneath his tongue. When he cradled Tuck's balls in one hand, Tuck moaned and thrust forward, pushing the shaft farther into Brendan's mouth.

Caught unaware, Brendan reared back, nearly gagging. He was annoyed with himself over this. He'd barely had more than the head past his lips. Both Jamie and Tuck had made it seem effortless—taking the shaft all the way to its base without so much as a flicker of their eyelids.

He leaned over Tuck's cock again, determined to do better. He licked at the spongy head and moved lower. This time he gripped the base of Tuck's shaft so he didn't have as far down to go. Tuck's appreciative moans spurred him on, giving him confidence.

He could do this. Why not? He wanted to give Tuck the incredible pleasure both Tuck and Jamie had given him. He lowered his head farther, using his tongue and lips as he moved. Tuck grabbed his head and thrust forward again, pushing his cock past Brendan's soft palate. Again Brendan gagged and pulled up sharply, gasping and silently cursing himself.

"You better sit tight, Tuck." Jamie's voice was teasing. "You're choking the guy with that huge dick of yours. Let him dictate the pace, why don't you?"

Brendan was at once grateful and irritated with Jamie's

remarks. It was hard enough to suck a guy's cock for the first time without a third party providing advice and running commentary.

"Shut up, he's doing great." Tuck's support made Brendan smile.

"Oh yeah? Gonna make me?" Jamie laughed.

"Yeah."

"How?"

"Like this." Tuck leaned toward Jamie and kissed him. Brendan sat back on his haunches watching them, his feelings hurtling from jealousy to voyeuristic pleasure to almost painful arousal. He stroked his cock as he watched them. After a moment he leaned down again, once more taking Tuck's shaft into his mouth.

Jamie's cock was pointing toward him as well and on an impulse Brendan grabbed it with one hand and began to stroke it. He kept his other hand on his own cock. Arrows of lust pierced him, shot directly from his groin, powered by what he was doing.

Tuck moaned against Jamie's mouth and put his hand on the back of Brendan's head. Brendan licked and sucked Tuck's long, thick shaft, dropping his own cock to fondle Tuck's balls. He kept his other hand firmly on Jamie, pulling against his erection until Jamie was panting.

When Brendan looked up, he saw they were no longer kissing. The two men were both leaning back on their hands, their legs parted wide and cocks thrust forward. Gaining in confidence, fueled by lust, Brendan swallowed more of Tuck's shaft and didn't gag at all.

"Brendan. Oh, God. Yes. So good, so good." Tuck's running litany was punctuated by Jamie's panting moans. Brendan could barely believe he was the one responsible for all this male pleasure. His cock throbbed at the realization.

All at once he felt Tuck stiffen, his balls tightening in Brendan's hand. Tuck shuddered and began to spurt in Brendan's mouth. The semen was bitter on his tongue and he jerked back, spitting.

Damn. He hated when women did that to him—pulled away just as he was coming. He forced himself to lower his head again, taking Tuck's member back into his mouth until Tuck's trembling shudders had subsided. He swallowed—it wasn't so bad now that he was expecting it.

He was still holding Jamie's cock and he focused his attention on the younger man, stroking and pulling the rock-hard shaft until Jamie came for the second time. Jamie fell back against the bed, joining Tuck.

Brendan sat in a sort of daze for a few moments. He, Brendan Aaronson, had just made two *guys* come!

"Where'd you find this dude, anyway, Tucker? He's not half bad."

"Had us fooled, didn't he? Pretending this was his first time and all."

Brendan growled with mock anger and hurled himself onto the two supine men. The three of them tumbled and laughed until they were breathless. Tuck held up his hands in surrender. "I'm a wounded man. Watch my stitches." The other two at once rolled away.

Brendan looked sharply at Tuck. They really should have been more careful around him. "I'm so *sorry.* Did we hurt you?"

Tuck, who had used the respite to climb over Brendan and catch him in a thigh lock, laughed. "Nah. I'm fine." Jamie, who apparently realized Tuck's ruse before Brendan, moved quickly to the head of the bed and grabbed Brendan's arms, pinning them beneath his knees.

"But you, my friend." Jamie's expression was deadpan, though his blue eyes twinkled. "You seem to be in something of a bind."

Brendan jerked beneath them but couldn't get a good angle to break free. A jolt of irrational fear surged through him at the realization he was trapped and at their mercy. His cock rose, even while his mind rebelled.

"Hey, let me go."

"You don't like being pinned down, huh? Helpless against two strong guys?" Tuck's tone was teasing, his dark eyes flashing.

Jamie leaned forward and flicked Brendan's telltale erection. "Me thinks the boy doth protest too much." He and Tuck laughed.

Brendan seized that moment to twist beneath them and get himself free. Then they were all laughing, moving together into each other's arms, barely aware of the screaming wind held at bay like starving wolves at their door.

Tuck sipped from a tall glass of rum and fresh pineapple juice served over crushed ice. The sand was pink, the white-tipped waves clear as green glass rolling over his feet. He closed his eyes and lifted his face to the welcoming sun.

"Yeah," he murmured, stroking the blond head in his lap. "That's good. Just like that." Warm lips closed over his cock, a wet tongue tickling its way down the shaft.

Tuck's eyes opened. Disoriented and confused, he looked around the stuffy, airless room. Where was the beach? The ocean? Brendan was sleeping beside him. He looked down to see Jamie between his legs. He stroked Jamie's hair. "Jamie, I thought I was dreaming."

Jamie released his cock and flashed him a dimpled grin. "Don't mind me. Go back to sleep." He ducked his head, bestowing wet kisses along the tops of Tuck's thighs. Each touch of his lips sent a shiver of pleasure through Tuck's loins.

"Sleep," Jamie whispered, pressing Tuck's legs apart to stroke his inner thighs. "Just ignore me."

For a few moments Tuck actually did drift between sleep and wakefulness, the sound of the ocean waves still crashing in his ears, though maybe it was just the wind. When Jamie gripped his balls in one hand and lowered his warm mouth onto Tuck's cock, he came more fully awake.

He groaned with pleasure. Jamie licked his way down the shaft and held the length of it deep in his throat for several seconds before gliding his lips upward. Jamie released Tuck's cock and scooted lower, licking in sensual circles around and between his balls, skating a figure eight of sensation over Tuck's nerve endings.

He wanted Jamie's mouth back on his cock. No, he wanted to bury his shaft deep in Jamie's tight little ass. Though Tuck liked to receive, he liked even better to give.

I want to fuck that tight, hot little ass.

Jamie lifted his head. "What did you say?"

Tuck was startled. "What?"

"I said, what did you say? Either I'm hearing things or you said, 'I want to fuck that tight, hot little ass.' Would that be my ass to which you are referring, Dr. Tucker?"

Flustered, Tuck put a hand over his face. "I didn't mean to say that out loud. I think I was still dreaming."

"You awake now?" Jamie was holding Tuck's cock in one

hand, an impish grin on his face.

"Uh, yeah."

"So, is that offer still good? Because I'm game."

Tuck glanced at the still-sleeping Brendan. "Right here? You have something?"

"Never leave home without them." Jamie laughed. "Got at least three in my wallet. Pre-lubricated and everything. And I wasn't even a Boy Scout."

Tuck found his mind at war with his body. He couldn't very well fuck Jamie with Brendan lying right beside them, could he? They could move to another cot, but what if Brendan woke up? Would he feel like they were sneaking around on him? What were the rules when it came to ménages, anyway? Should they wake Brendan to see if he wanted to join in?

Jamie, apparently oblivious to Tuck's protocol concerns, slipped naked from the bed and hurried over to the trunk at the end of his cot. He withdrew a slim red leather wallet and opened it, pulling out and waving a strip of condoms with a triumphant grin.

Brendan chose that moment to wake up. "Hey, what's going on?" He stretched and smiled sleepily at Tuck. "Did I miss breakfast?"

"Depends what you're hungry for," Tuck quipped, brandishing his erect cock toward Brendan with an evil grin. It tickled Tuck to think even after the hours-long orgy of the night before, Brendan was still shy enough to blush.

Jamie bounded back to the bed, eager as a frisky puppy. "Morning, sleepyhead." He smiled to Brendan, whose eyes traveled down first to Jamie's cock and then to what he held in his hand. Jamie, seeing the direction of his stare, held out his offering, palm up.

"Tuck's going to have his way with me. I tried to resist but he's bigger and stronger, so I gave in. Want to watch? Better yet, want to participate?"

Brendan's eyes were wide as plates and now his mouth opened as well. He looked at Tuck, back at Jamie and then to Tuck again. "You're going to...?"

Tuck tried and failed to get a read on Brendan's reaction. Was he excited by the idea? Turned off? Jealous? Hoping it was the former, suspecting it was also the latter and praying it wasn't the one in between, he put his hand on Brendan's shoulder and leaned over to kiss his cheek.

"Would you like to see how it's done? Maybe join in if you feel comfortable?"

Brendan's cock was rising like a windsock, despite his protest. "Oh, um. I don't think I could..."

"You didn't think you could do any of this before we started, did you?" Jamie stared pointedly at Brendan's undeniable erection. "And now look at you. I bet you could hammer a nail with that thing."

Brendan's cheeks were scarlet. Jamie was relentless with his teasing. To give Brendan a break as much as anything, Tuck tackled Jamie, grabbing him around the waist and pulling him down onto the cot. He began to tickle Jamie, running his fingers mercilessly over Jamie's bare sides and digging in. Jamie laughed while trying to shield himself with his hands, but Tuck showed him no mercy.

Joining in, Brendan leaned over and grabbed Jamie's wrists, pulling his arms taut overhead. "There you go, Tuck. Let's teach this mouthy boy a thing or two."

Jamie was writhing beneath them, laughing hysterically, tears spilling down his cheeks. "Stop—" he gasped. "No more...I'll be good, I swear..."

After several more minutes of torturing poor Jamie, they relented. Brendan let go of his wrists and Tuck sat back, folding his arms over his chest. He stared down at Jamie, assuming a mock-stern expression that slid into a grin despite his best efforts. "Stop teasing Dr. Aaronson. He's your team leader, don't forget. Show a little respect."

Jamie, still gasping for breath, nodded as he wiped tears of laughter from his cheeks. Tuck noticed his cock wasn't as erect as before. No doubt he was distracted by the tickling. Deciding to remedy that, he grabbed Jamie's cock and pulled, jerking the loose skin upward. He gripped hard on purpose, having noted the night before Jamie's intense sexual reaction to mild erotic pain.

As he expected, Jamie drew in his breath at the rough treatment. His cock hardened in Tuck's grip and he thrust his hips upward. "You like it rough, hmm, Jamie?" Tuck found himself aroused by Jamie's ardent response. His own cock had regained its former prowess.

Jamie didn't answer. Tuck jerked harder at his erection, thrilling to Jamie's reaction. "Yes," Jamie whispered raggedly. "Please."

The mood shifted. Gone was the playful atmosphere of a moment before. Power flowed like liquid fire through Tuck's veins. He released Jamie's bone-hard erection.

He looked at Brendan, who was watching them. Tuck's surging power rush was checked by the look in Brendan's eyes—half desire, half pleading.

He leaned close, his mouth near Brendan's ear. "You okay? I want to fuck Jamie, but I want you to be a part of this."

Brendan nodded, his eyes fixing on Jamie, who lay inert beside him, his cock still caught in Tuck's grip.

"I want to try something." Tuck rolled from the cot to the

floor and knelt facing the other two. "Brendan, you kneel up on the bed facing us. Jamie, you get on your knees facing Brendan, your ass as close to the edge of the cot as you can get."

He held his breath, waiting to see if they would obey. He was reasonably sure Jamie would, but Brendan remained the unknown quantity. He was both pleased and relieved when Jamie scrambled upright and Brendan scooted back. He knelt as directed, his erect cock thick and hard between his legs.

Jamie shifted to a kneeling position, the globes of his tight, sexy ass splayed over the edge of the cot. They knelt waiting, face-to-face, cock-to-cock. Tuck picked up the strip of condoms, tore open one of the packets and rolled the pre-lubricated sheath over his cock.

He moved closer, pointing his cock toward Jamie's offered ass. Though the cot was lower to the ground than a regular bed, he wanted better access. "Give me those pillows."

Brendan, following his gaze, tossed the three pillows toward Tuck. He positioned them beneath his knees. The added height was perfect for penetration.

But not yet. First Tuck licked his finger and ran it around the rim of Jamie's dark pink puckered hole. He pushed a finger inside. Jamie grunted and pushed back against him, causing the finger to sink in to the second knuckle. Tuck inserted another finger beside the first, moving them inside Jamie's tight ass until the muscles relaxed.

Tuck looked at Brendan. His face was flushed, his blond hair tousled, his eyes glittering in the glow of the nightlight. Tuck almost forgot Jamie as he stared into them. Brendan swallowed, his Adam's apple bobbing, his tongue appearing on his lower lip.

His balls aching, Tuck turned his attentions back to Jamie,

adding a third finger to the stretching orifice. With his other hand, Tuck gripped Jamie's balls from behind and squeezed. Jamie groaned and wriggled back wantonly against Tuck's hand.

Satisfied he was ready, Tuck removed his fingers and positioned himself behind Jamie, the head of his cock nudging between Jamie's cheeks. He withdrew it a moment, spit on his fingers and rubbed them along the condom, hoping the pre-lube plus his saliva would be sufficient to keep Jamie comfortable.

Repositioning himself, he teased the entrance with the tip of his cock until Jamie pushed back against him, causing the head of his cock to penetrate. He pressed forward, reveling in the grip of Jamie's tight ass. He was careful at first, giving him a chance to adjust, but Jamie pushed back again, forcing Tuck's cock deeper.

Tuck craned his head around Jamie's broad back and what he saw made him catch his breath. It was even better than he'd hoped. Brendan's hand was wrapped around Jamie's shaft, Jamie's on his. They were pumping each other's cock with rhythmic strokes.

"Jesus, you two are hot," Tuck breathed. He couldn't see Jamie's face, but Brendan turned to look at him, his eyes blazing with pure lust. Tuck rested his cheek against Jamie's shoulder, keeping his eyes on Brendan as he eased himself all the way inside the hot passageway.

Jamie's ass held him like a vise, the pleasure almost excruciatingly acute as he moved in and out of the tight hole. Jamie began to pant, his body quivering and jerking with each thrust. Brendan brought his arms around Jamie, pulling him into a strong embrace. Jamie, likewise, dropped Brendan's cock and put his arms around him.

Tuck, his cock buried inside Jamie, brought his arms

around the pair as well, sandwiching Jamie between them. Brendan leaned forward until his face was close enough to touch.

Tuck kissed Brendan, pummeling Jamie's ass while his tongue danced with Brendan's. Jamie was moaning, trapped between the two strong men. He let his head fall back on Tuck's shoulder, his body convulsing against the relentless onslaught.

Tuck began to shudder, on the edge of orgasm though he didn't want to stop. He didn't ever want to stop. Life could suspend at this precise instant in time, with him buried deep in Jamie's hot ass, his tongue down Brendan's throat, the three of them locked together in the most intimate of embraces.

His body took over however, dragging him into a climax that started in his toes and ripped through his body like a freight train. He slumped against Jamie, his heart threatening to beat through the wall of his chest, the blood roaring in his ears. He was vaguely aware of Jamie's body spasming beneath his.

When he could catch his breath, he moved back, careful to keep the condom in place as he withdrew. He looked across at the two men, both still breathing heavily.

Jamie gave a small, embarrassed laugh. "Oops, I did it again." He slid from Brendan's lap to sit beside him and Tuck realized what had happened. No doubt the friction of his cock mashed up against Brendan's body, coupled with Tuck's cock thrusting into him had sent Jamie over the edge. Tuck saw both Brendan and Jamie's stomachs were smeared with the evidence of Jamie's release.

Using the edge of a sheet, Jamie wiped his belly and turned to do the same for Brendan. "No." Tuck's tone held command. "Lick it off."

Jamie turned to stare at him, his expression inscrutable.

131

Tuck waited to see how he would react, keeping his own face impassive. After a beat, Jamie slipped from the cot to kneel beside Tuck. Leaning forward, he snaked out his tongue, touching its tip to the white ribbon of come dripping down Brendan's stomach.

Pressing his tongue flat, he licked in a long, hard line toward Brendan's erection, not stopping until he reached the shaft. Brendan moaned and leaned back on his hands, his head falling back, as Jamie slid his tongue along the shaft and closed his lips over the head of the cock.

Tuck dipped his head beneath Jamie's, licking at Brendan's balls. *"Christ."* The word was wrenched from Brendan between gasps of pleasure. Within less than a minute, he cried out, his fingers twisting in Jamie's hair, his hips thrusting upward in orgasm.

Tuck didn't stop licking Brendan's balls until Jamie had sucked every last drop from him. Jamie was smiling baby-wide toward Brendan, but Brendan's eyes were fixed on Tuck. His expression was at once so fierce and yet so tender it made Tuck's heart skip a beat. Was this what love felt like?

Chapter Eleven

At first no one reacted to the sound. Jamie was the first to move. It was only reluctantly that Brendan tore his gaze from Tuck's handsome face. If he'd had his choice, he would have lain there forever, just staring at its planes and contours, committing each feature to memory.

But the phone was ringing.

The phone was ringing!

Jamie, already halfway across the room, hurtled toward the card table, on which the cell phone was jangling. "Jamie Hunter." He held his breath, listened and nodded, turning wide, excited eyes toward the other two.

"Yes. Yes, excellent. Okay. Keep us posted. We'll be ready. Thank you. Oh, God, thank you so much." There were tears in Jamie's eyes. He stood naked, the cell phone in his hand, his hair wild and hanging in his face.

"They're coming. They said the worst is over. The winds have died down enough to get a helicopter over from McMurdo Air Force Base. They have a cargo plane there that can take us to New Zealand. We're really lucky because they're closing down in a few days. If this blizzard had kept it up a while longer, we'd be spending a long, dark winter in this godforsaken place."

The incredibly sensual, hot mood seemed to chill and evaporate like so much ice vapor in the wind. Tuck was moving quickly, pulling on underwear and reaching for his jeans. "When are they coming? How long do we have?"

"They hope within the hour. They'll call again to make sure we can get out of the building."

Brendan sat up, the sensual net that had been thrown over him burning away at last as he absorbed the full implications of what was going on. It was over. They were being rescued. They would all be going home. Tuck and Jamie to California, he back to Washington State.

"Come on, Bren." Tuck's tone was affectionate but there was urgency beneath it. "Get your sexy ass moving. We've got to pack what we can fit in rucksacks, shut down the generator, bundle ourselves up and see if we can't get outside again. As hot as you look lying there butt naked, we've got to get cracking."

Brendan stood abruptly. Tuck was right. There was a lot to do. They wouldn't want to keep a hovering helicopter waiting. He headed to the bathroom. He would have liked to shower, but settled for splashing water over his face and chest.

Jesus, had that really happened? In light of the impending rescue, Brendan couldn't decide how he felt. Looking at himself in the mirror as he dried his face, he shook his head. He wasn't gay. He couldn't be falling in love with another *man*. Or, for that matter, two men. Could he?

Okay, so maybe he was bi. Or bi-curious. Yes, that was more accurate, and being a scientist, naturally he wanted to be accurate, even where emotions and sexuality were concerned. Only, if he were honest, his curiosity wasn't satisfied—not by a long shot.

Yet surely it was only because of the extreme situation in which they'd found themselves that the whole crazy scene had happened at all. That and enough liquor to pickle a healthy liver. It never would have happened in normal circumstances.

Well, things were returning to normal, weren't they? In a few short hours they'd be at McMurdo, and from there back to civilization. Back to a life that didn't include Tuck or Jamie. He would return to his lab, his teaching, his dull, contained, controlled little world.

"Hurry up, Brendan. We're both packed. Get a move on." Jamie, who was nearly ten years Brendan's junior and a mere lab assistant, was out there shouting orders like he owned the place. Instead of being annoyed, Brendan grinned with affection. He was going to miss the hell out of him.

Jamie was fully dressed. Both his and Tuck's rucksacks were crammed with the contents of their storage trunks. Brendan moved to his trunk, grabbing armfuls of clothing and shoving them carelessly into his bag. He shut down his laptop and carefully placed it into its case, slipping the backup memory stick that contained a copy of all his raw data and research into his pocket.

Tuck emerged from the kitchen. "Should we take a couple of energy bars for the road?"

"If I never see another fucking energy bar, it will be too soon." Jamie laughed.

Brendan turned off the space heaters. Almost at once the room began to cool. At least the wind was no longer buffeting the building. In fact, it was eerily quiet. Brendan felt unsettled and out of sorts. He looked around the room, telling himself it was because he didn't yet believe they were really being rescued, but in his heart he knew otherwise.

Their gear in tow, the three men moved into the kitchen, where they suited up in their outer pants, boots, scarves, gloves and parkas, their mittens shoved into their pockets.

They walked down the hallway, flashlights at the ready,

135

stopping first at the generator shed. "Guess they'll have to fix that one next summer," Tuck remarked. Brendan, recalling the bright red blood splattered over the floor and covering half of Tuck's face, suppressed a shudder.

His usual ruddy color had returned. He looked fit, the only evidence of his fall the bandage still covering the stitches. Thank God he was okay. *I don't want to leave him.* Brendan pushed the thought away.

Tuck moved forward to flick the off switch and the rumbling engine died. Flashlights guiding the way, they entered the lab where Jamie and Brendan had made their first escape, deciding to go with a route they already knew worked.

The pale light of the waning sun backlit the cloud-covered sky. Soon that sun would dip permanently below the horizon for the next hundred days or so, plunging the continent into an eternal night.

The cell phone rang in Brendan's pocket and he pulled it out. "Brendan Aaronson."

"The helicopter will be there in about five minutes. They won't be able to land, but they'll drop a sling harness and airlift you one at a time. You all ready?"

"Yeah, we're ready to get the hell out of here," Brendan asserted, ignoring the whisper of aching sadness deep in his heart.

They managed to push the window open. A drift of snow fell into the room. Donning their mittens, they brushed the sill clear and climbed out, one at a time, into the freezing air.

Their gear hoisted over their backs, they waded through the snow toward the side of the building nearest the landing strip and waited, no one speaking. Within a few minutes the sound of the chopper was audible and in a moment it appeared against the blanket of blinding white snow that stretched as far as the eye could see.

It hovered overhead, the wind from the propellers stirring up the air and sending sharp needles of icy snow spraying into their faces. The door on the side of the helicopter opened and Brendan saw the winch, on which was wound thick, sturdy cable, a horse-collar rescue sling attached.

"You go first," he shouted to Tuck, concerned about his bandaged head in the biting cold. Tuck nodded and moved forward. He passed the sling under his arms and gave a signal for them to raise him. Brendan watched him being lifted from the ground, unaware that tears had gathered in his eyes until they spilled, freezing at once along his cheeks. He told himself they were tears of joy.

Chapter Twelve

"Brendan, you're not listening to me."

Brendan looked across the table, guilty as charged. "What? I'm sorry. I was thinking about something."

"Let me guess, the microbial composition of a deep ice core?" Lynn, like Brendan, was a researcher at the Kramer Institute of Science located in the University District of Seattle. Once engaged, they'd broken it off by mutual agreement the year before. They'd made a point of remaining friends, but since he'd returned from Antarctica, Lynn had been eager to rekindle the flames and Brendan, confused and lonely, had let her.

They were sitting in Brendan's kitchen over a breakfast of homemade pancakes, bacon and scrambled eggs Lynn had destroyed Brendan's kitchen preparing and for which Brendan had no appetite. He smiled distractedly. "Something like that."

"Well, I'd appreciate it if you listen to me when I'm talking. This is a big deal to me. Pratt thinks I'm going to get this grant, but without the proper backing from the NSF, there's no way it's going to happen."

Brendan tried to focus on what Lynn was saying. She was an attractive woman, petite, with thick, dark hair and large brown eyes. He had once thought he loved her, though he'd never, he now knew, connected with her.

Not on the gut level he'd connected with Tuck, where words

weren't even necessary and more was shared through one kiss than all the conversation of a lifetime. Jesus, he missed Tuck. He missed Jamie too, he wouldn't deny it. Jamie, with that long hair flopping over into those baby blues, his mouth twisting up into a sardonic smile. He thought about the snake tattoo, the physical symbol of the bad boy behind the earnest research scientist persona they had all worn during the project's duration. Who really knew a person? Brendan hadn't even known himself.

"Damn it, you still haven't heard a word I'm saying. I could be talking to the wall. Now I remember why we broke up the first time." Lynn's voice, normally a pleasing register, had risen to a piercing shrill.

Brendan looked at her again, suppressing a sigh. It had been a mistake to let her back into his life, or more accurately, into his bed. If he were honest, he knew why he'd done it. He had to see, to know if he'd been ruined by...

He wouldn't even let himself articulate the thought. There was nothing wrong with being gay. He'd done nothing wrong by experimenting with the guys. Of course, it would never have happened in a normal situation. It was the backdrop of danger, the possibility they might not be rescued in time, which had lowered his defenses, made him do things and accept things he would never have even considered in a normal situation.

That didn't make him gay, just human.

When he'd returned to Seattle, Lynn had been the one waiting for him at the airport. He'd expected Charlie, his best friend at Kramer, but Lynn, he'd later found out from Charlie, had convinced him to let her go in his stead. She had realized, she told Brendan, when she heard about his being stranded, that she had never stopped loving him and wanted to try again.

He kept her at arm's length for a few days, pleading

139

exhaustion, and she'd been gracious enough. She'd also been persistent, showing up at his place night after night with casseroles in her arms and skimpy lingerie beneath her clothes. In his usual passive fashion, Brendan had eventually gone along, allowing her back into his bed after only a week of solicitous attention and courtship on her part.

At night when they made love and her mouth closed over his cock, he couldn't help but compare her talents to those of Tuck and Jamie. She was technically capable, but the passion, the fierce, lusty joy both men had brought to the task made her efforts seem clinical and even boring.

He knew that wasn't entirely fair. He didn't love her, so the experience had been empty, a mere physical exchange. But did that mean he loved the two men? Could a person fall in love in the space of a few days? No—surely it was just the excitement of something new, something forbidden, that had added the intense overlay of passion he'd felt in their arms.

With Lynn he felt guilty and strange, aware it was the memories of Tuck and Jamie playing through his mind that kept his cock hard in her mouth, rather than any real desire for her. When she lay back against his sheets, her pretty body bare for him, nipples erect, legs spread, he'd moved willingly enough over her, relieved he could still get and maintain an erection with a woman.

That proved he wasn't gay, didn't it?

He'd been right to refuse Tuck's overtures when he'd called the week before, suggesting the three of them get together. He could just imagine Tuck and Jamie, who lived and worked in Monterey and probably had already moved in together, the perfect gay couple. How could he compete with that? Why would he even want to? His life was here; his work was here.

It was better to put the bizarre events of that strange time behind him. He had to move on—return to the real world, focus on his research. It had hurt to hear the pain in Tuck's voice when he had had to explain that whatever had happened between them couldn't be real, that it was better to nip it in the bud. He'd done the right thing.

Lynn stood abruptly, pushing her chair back from the table so it nearly toppled. "I've got to go. You obviously don't give two shits about my grant." Her voice was ripe with reproach. She glared at his plate, still heaped with the mound of eggs and pancakes she'd placed before him. "Or my breakfast." He looked up at her, trying to muster some kind of emotion, waiting for the next sentence that was bound to follow, and did. "Or *me.*"

"You're brooding about the phone call, aren't you?"

They were sitting on Jamie's front porch, shaded by tall cypress trees, enjoying the fresh sea air and the prospect of the weekend stretching out before them. Tuck was staring out at the Pacific and Jamie could tell by the look in his eyes he was thinking about Brendan.

"Yeah." Tuck's voice was sad. "I can't believe he actually spouted that shit about soldiers comforting each other during trench warfare. Jesus. Do you think he really buys his own crap?"

Jamie shook his head, forcing down the irritation he felt. He missed Brendan too, far more than he'd expected, but Tuck's obsession was getting a little old. They still had each other, didn't they? Wasn't that enough?

It had been strange, though in retrospect not surprising, to watch Brendan metamorphose before their eyes back into the straight, uptight, closed-off man he'd been before the blizzard had blown his carefully constructed heterosexual world apart.

All three of them had been discreet, naturally, during their brief stay at McMurdo and their flight out to Christchurch. They hadn't had much chance to interact in New Zealand before being flown back to California.

Tuck had been kept overnight in a medical facility to check for concussion and see to his head wound, which had healed remarkably well. Brendan and Jamie were given separate rooms at the military compound, but they'd shared meals and leisure time together. When Jamie had tried to talk, even in the vaguest terms, about what had gone on between them, Brendan had shut down tighter than a clam, his discomfort painfully obvious.

There hadn't been seats for the three of them to sit together on the flight to California, which was just as well, as Jamie hadn't been in the mood for Brendan's monosyllabic responses and Tuck's wounded expression. He'd slept most of the twelve-hour flight, dreaming of his own bed, blue California skies, the ocean and the carne asada burritos and homemade tortillas at his favorite Mexican restaurant by the bay.

In the airport, they'd said their goodbyes, Brendan stiffly, Tuck with his heart on his sleeve. Brendan had a connecting flight to Seattle and Jamie, by that point, had been glad to see the back of him.

Tuck and he had been met by Landon Smith and Stuart Baker, both high up in the chain of command at Wexler. Jamie had been dropped home first, though he hadn't wanted to leave Tuck. Tuck had climbed out of the car with him and Jamie had almost begged him not to go.

"I'll call you as soon as I get home," Tuck whispered, hugging him tight as their bosses watched impassively from inside the car.

True to his word, he had called, and came that very night to Jamie's cottage and to his bed. In the two months they'd been home, Tuck had barely returned to his small apartment near California State, where he taught science courses to augment his research salary at the institute.

Jamie could never have afforded his Carmel cottage by the sea on his paltry salary from Wexler. Happily, he had no mortgage. He'd inherited the place from his great uncle who had died two years before. Uncle Frank had been a closet homosexual until his seventies, when he finally came out and admitted what everyone already knew—his roommate of the last forty years was in fact his lover.

At least Uncle Frank, unlike Brendan, hadn't hidden the truth from *himself*. While Jamie was frustrated and saddened by Brendan's defection, which is what it felt like to him, he was most pissed off because of the way it hurt Tuck. Tuck, who had carried secret feelings for Brendan for nearly a year, was having a much harder time putting the guy out of his mind and heart.

"Let it go, Tuck." Jamie kept his voice gentle as he touched Tuck's arm.

"Yeah, you're right. He's not worth the energy," Tuck asserted. Jamie eyed him, aware Tuck hadn't finished expending that energy, but there wasn't much he could do about it. Tuck brightened suddenly. "Hey. Want your present now or later?"

Jamie beamed, warmth spreading through him. He hadn't mentioned that it was his twenty-sixth birthday—birthdays were for children. Nevertheless he felt absurdly happy that Tuck had somehow found out. "You got me a present? How did you know?"

"I'm a research scientist. The first night I came over I

researched the driver's license you left on the bureau."

Jamie laughed and followed Tuck into the house. Tuck went to his backpack and took out a small oblong box wrapped in silver paper. He handed it to Jamie. Inside was an inch-long coiled snake of hammered gold.

"Wow, that's beautiful." Jamie lifted the piece of jewelry from the box and held it up. Its emerald green eyes glittered in the light.

"It's one of a kind. I thought you could wear it on your gold chain. Want to try it on?"

"Sure." Jamie reached for the chain he wore around his neck and released the clasp.

"Take off your shirt too." Tuck's grin was sly. "We can see it better that way."

"One track mind," Jamie teased, though he was happy enough to obey. Sex with Tuck had continued to be fantastic, especially lately. Tuck, rightly sensing Jamie's as yet mostly unexplored submissive tendencies, had become increasingly dominant during sex, with explosive results.

They walked into the bedroom so Jamie could see the effect in the mirror. Tuck stood behind him, admiring the snake that rested against his sternum, a jeweled twin to the snake tattoo on his hip.

"Now you get your second present."

Jamie grinned, assuming Tuck meant sex, but to his surprise, Tuck pulled another, smaller box out of his jeans pocket and held it out. It wasn't wrapped. Jamie opened the lid. Inside was a clear silicone cuff that covered a series of large pearls. He lifted it from the box and raised his eyebrows.

"Is this what I think it is?"

"And what would that be?" Tuck's grin was mischievous.

"A cock ring?" He squeezed it, feeling the hard pearls trapped in the rubbery silicone.

"You got it. It'll keep you nice and hard while I fuck that hot ass of yours."

Jamie's cock rose at once to the challenge. "Hey, I'm game."

"I knew you would be. Not that you have a choice in the matter. It's what *I* want."

Jamie felt the hot, slow surge of blood ripple through his veins. This always happened when Tuck assumed his Dom persona. Colors somehow became brighter, sensations more intense, desire heightened.

He stepped out of his jeans and underwear. Tuck held out his palm and Jamie dropped the cock ring onto it. Tuck knelt before him and gripped Jamie's erection in his large hand. "Since you're already hard, we'll just slip it over the shaft for now. Later I want to try it behind your balls."

Tuck tugged at the cock ring, pulling it wider. "That's the cool thing about this ring. It's stretchy, so it can fit over an erect cock. 'Cause that's your perennial state, isn't it, Jamie?"

"Around you it is," Jamie admitted with a grin. He watched as Tuck slipped the beaded ring along his shaft. When he had rolled it to the base, he let it go. The ring's grip was snug but not painful. It forced his cock to point straight out from his groin, the trapped blood engorging it even more than normal.

"*Very* nice." Tuck stood back to admire his handiwork. Unable to resist, Jamie stroked his shaft, which was taut beneath his fingers.

Tuck leaned forward and slapped his hand away. "Uh-unh. That's my cock. You can look but you can't touch. Put your hands behind your back and don't move."

Jamie pretended to pout, though he loved every second of

it. Tuck, so easygoing most of the time, was masterful in the bedroom. Tuck knelt in front of him and lovingly took him into his mouth, stroking his balls as he worshiped Jamie's cock until his knees threatened to buckle.

Tuck pulled back. "Don't you dare come. Not yet. I want to fuck you first." He led Jamie to the bed. "Lie on your back so I can see that sexy cock ring and the look in your eyes when I shove my cock up your ass."

Jamie obeyed, his cock pointing straight to the ceiling.

Quickly Tuck shucked his clothing and slipped a condom in place on his own cock. He crouched on the bed between Jamie's legs and pushed them up until Jamie's heels were touching his ass. He scooted down, spreading Jamie's ass cheeks.

Jamie sighed with pleasure as Tuck's tongue rimmed his asshole in a slow, sensual circle. After a moment the tongue was replaced with fingers made gooey with lubricant and after that, the head of his thick, long cock.

Tuck leaned up over him, balancing his weight on his hands as if he were going to do pushups. He moved forward, pressing his girth into Jamie's willing body, not stopping until their balls touched.

Lowering himself, he kissed Jamie on the lips as he thrust forward, deep in Jamie's tight passage. Jamie groaned against his mouth. His cock was massaged by Tuck's body as he moved back and forth inside of him.

At first Tuck fucked him slow and easy, lulling him into an erotic trance. "Feels so good," Tuck whispered. "So good inside you. Yeah..." He began to move faster, his head back, the tendons on his neck standing out. Though it was only sixty degrees outside, the air in the room felt hot, Tuck's body like a furnace over him.

Tuck picked up the tempo, slamming into him, forcing a grunt from Jamie's lips with each thrust. He loved the feeling of being so full, so possessed by another person. It was especially intimate to have Tuck facing him, the angle permitting deep penetration.

He brought his arms around Tuck, pulling him closer. He bit Tuck's muscular shoulder to distract himself from ejaculating before Tuck did. Tuck began to tremble, his body covered in sweat, his breath a pant. Jamie could feel him coming inside him and he clenched his muscles as best he could from his position, milking Tuck's cock as he climaxed.

Tuck fell heavily against him, his cock sliding out of Jamie's ass. He pulled himself up over Jamie and then rolled beside him, using a tissue to remove and toss the spent condom. Turning back to Jamie, he grabbed his stiff erection. The ring at its base gripped him tight and his cock was nearly purple and very sensitive to the touch.

"Poor baby," Tuck murmured in a low, sensual voice. "Your cock looks like it's going to explode if it doesn't get some attention."

Jamie didn't deny this. He put his hands beneath his head so he could watch while Tuck lowered his dark head over Jamie's groin, taking his ringed cock into his mouth.

It didn't take long for Jamie to near the edge. Tuck had his balls in one hand, his cock deep in his throat. He pulled back only long enough to issue a command. "Come for me."

Jamie did.

Dinner had been nice, a romantic affair at an outside café

on the bay, the sun setting like liquid gold over the water, Jamie's blue eyes shining in the candlelight wavering on their table.

They'd gone back to Jamie's cottage to make slow, sensual love for several more hours. Jamie was asleep in his bed, a satisfied smile on his lips, but Tuck couldn't sleep. He sat on the porch, listening to the lulling crash of the waves, a glass of red wine in his hand, staring off into the middle distance.

He'd brought out a pad of paper and a pen, with the intention of writing out a To Do list for the following week, hoping this would distract him sufficiently to get his mind off Brendan Aaronson, at least for a while. Brendan, or rather the loss of him, was like losing a tooth, the tongue drawn inexorably to the place that shouldn't be empty, but was.

He'd almost called him a dozen times, after that first and only devastating call, when Brendan had basically denied everything Tuck knew to be true. First pride, then anger, then resignation had all colluded to keep him from trying again. Jamie was right. If Brendan wanted to live in denial, that was his problem, not theirs. They had each other, without the need to lie or pretend.

Tuck had to admit he was falling in love with Jamie. They'd connected on so many levels in the time since they'd been back in California. It was ironic to realize they'd worked in the same building for over a year and had barely exchanged more than a few words prior to the Antarctica adventure. Jamie's excellent research reputation had preceded him, which was why Tuck had recommended him for the project, but socially he'd basically dismissed Jamie as just another pretty boy, too young to be worth noticing.

How wrong he had been. Jamie was the most emotionally honest of the three of them, and the most willing to put himself at risk in matters of the heart. Beneath the dry humor and the sometimes swaggering bad-boy persona, Jamie was a bright, sensitive, romantic man. On top of that, he was sexually insatiable, with a delicious submissive streak Tuck found erotic as hell.

He had Jamie, wasn't that enough?

Let it go, Jamie had wisely advised him. After all, what had they really had with Brendan? A few days of crazed sex did not a relationship make. Why was he wasting his time and energy obsessing about the guy, especially when he'd made it clear he wanted nothing more to do with them?

Maybe Brendan was right—what they'd shared had been nothing more than the acting out of three frightened guys trying to deal with the possibility of being stranded without adequate provisions for the duration of a brutal Antarctic winter.

Brendan had been bi-curious, nothing more. And obviously, that curiosity had been more than satisfied in those few days. Whatever emotional connection Tuck had thought they'd forged, it had apparently been one-sided.

Well, two-sided. And as Jamie had joked, two out of three ain't bad.

It should have been enough. They'd been rescued. He'd been given a clean bill of health after a fall that could have killed him, if the guys hadn't found him before the CO fumes did him in. He'd found a new love in Jamie, one he never expected.

If they'd left with the rest of the research crew, he would have continued to think of Jamie as just another junior researcher at the institute. He would have continued to make the erroneous and unfair assumption that because Jamie was young and good looking, that he was also shallow and boring, and not worth Tuck's time or attention.

Instead he'd found a wonderful lover and companion in Jamie, who wisely advised him to let Brendan and the whole ménage thing go. Jamie was able to move past it, so why couldn't he? What was it about Brendan that wouldn't let him go?

What was it about Brendan that had kept him interested for the entire year after their first meeting up in Washington State? Even then, before he'd tasted his sweet lips or sucked his hard cock, Tuck had felt a deep, abiding, kindred connection with Brendan for which he had no rational explanation or words.

When those gray green eyes fixed on his, Tuck felt as if the world stopped. Time no longer mattered, gravity was irrelevant, life narrowed and focused to just the two of them. Would he never see those eyes again? That sunny, wide smile that made his heart catch? Would he never touch Brendan's sexy, muscular thighs or lick his thick, straight shaft and the warm balls beneath?

Tuck glanced down at his pad. He'd been scrawling words without realizing it. When he saw what he had written, he tore off the page in anger, bunched it into a ball and tossed it over the side of the porch.

The night air was chilling him and he was tired. There was a good, sexy man waiting in bed to take him into his arms. Life was what it was, not what he wished it would be. He would count his blessings and take what was given him. Brendan could go to hell.

Chapter Thirteen

Brendan unlocked the door to his house, glancing furtively from left to right. He had to laugh at himself. Like anyone gave a shit what he was carrying in the plain brown paper bag. It wasn't illegal, it wasn't even particularly risqué.

Still, it wasn't like him to frequent an adult sex shop. He hadn't ventured into one in years. On his way to work every morning he passed through a seedy neighborhood with a small strip shopping center that included a Chinese takeout place, a discount shoe store, a tobacco shop, two boarded-up storefronts and the Purple Passion Adult Bookstore.

There were perhaps three books in the whole store, but there were plenty of sex toys, including blowup dolls with tight Os for mouths, dildos in a bewildering array of materials and sizes, lubricants in all flavors and colors, candy underpants, gags, whips, handcuffs and an extensive library of X-Rated DVDs and old used videotapes with sticky covers.

He'd found what he was looking for and bought it, glad the cashier, a large, slovenly man in a stained shirt, hadn't made eye contact during the transaction. He was both eager and nervous at the prospect of trying it out. He would have a glass of scotch on the rocks first, to unwind.

Jesus. A date with yourself. Drinks first, then sex. How pathetic you are, Aaronson.

Since Lynn, along with the diet of steady sex she had provided, was no longer in the picture or in his bed, Brendan had begun to have dreams at night. Vivid, darkly erotic dreams in which both Tuck and Jamie loomed large.

He would awaken in a sweat, his hand on his erect cock, his heart thumping. Sometimes the dreams went so far he even awoke to find he'd ejaculated in his sleep. He hadn't had wet dreams since college.

After Lynn had stormed out, he had called her, apologizing for his behavior. She'd forced the issue, demanding that he either commit to their relationship going forward, or call it quits. As gently as he could, he chose the latter option, assuring her the problem wasn't with her, but with himself.

Which was true. Woefully, abysmally true. He found himself no longer fit for the love of a woman, but too unsure and confused to accept the love of a man. Not that that love was being offered any longer. He'd had his chance with Tuck and Jamie. He'd soundly, royally, completely fucked it up.

Too terrified to confront his own unresolved issues and desires, he'd glibly dismissed Tuck when he'd called, condescendingly explaining that what the three of them had shared over the course of a few crazy, wildly intense days had been the stuff of fantasies. It wasn't something that could be sustained back in the real world.

They'd had their fun, now life was supposed to resume as normal. *Normal*, he thought bitterly. *What the fuck is normal?*

He'd been fooling himself. The realization was frightening. He had clung to the idea he could *will* himself into normalcy. That was why he'd let Lynn back into his life in the first place, even while in the back of his mind he knew it was a mistake. She was to have been his front, the proof he was straight. And for a while he'd actually pulled it off, or so he'd thought, nearly blotting out the crushing melancholy that lingered just below the surface of his so-called normal life.

Once inside the house, he grabbed the bottle of scotch from the liquor cabinet, put ice into a glass and took bottle and glass, along with the paper bag, into the living room. He poured himself several ounces of liquor and drank it down. Setting the bottle and glass on the coffee table, he opened the paper bag and took out the slim black rubber dildo and the tube of KY Jelly inside.

He wanted to know what it felt like. That was all. The dreams, the ones that made him come in his sleep, had invariably included either Tuck or Jamie penetrating him. They had been powerful dreams, filled with both fear and ecstasy.

In the magical way of dreams, he'd been both the giver and the receiver. It was as if he'd had two cocks, the one in his ass and the one in Tuck or Jamie's mouth, depending on the scenario. He could *feel* their pleasure along with his own. He could feel the hot grip of muscle massaging his cock, tighter than any pussy could be. At the same time, he felt full, filled, fulfilled, when taken by one of his lovers.

His *lovers.*

He poured a second scotch and drank it quickly, wanting to be drunk, needing to be drunk. Without even bothering to go into the bedroom, he kicked off his shoes and stripped off his pants and underwear. He leaned back against the sofa, his bare ass making contact with the cool leather.

He hadn't masturbated since the rescue. He knew why now—he was afraid of his own fantasies. Afraid of the images he knew would fill his head when he did. "Admit it. Just fucking admit it, Aaronson. You want them. Both of them. You need them. You *are* them."

He realized he was talking out loud. Well, so what? He was

allowed to talk out loud in his own damn house. He was allowed to shove a dildo up his ass if he felt like it. It didn't make him...

Disgusted with himself, Brendan again spoke to the empty room. "Your problem is labels. You have to assign a name and a rationale to every damn thing. You have to posit a hypothesis and then set about proving or disproving it. Life *isn't* a fucking science lab. Tuck and Jamie aren't defined by who they love. Why should you be?"

He lifted the bottle of liquor and took a swig, no longer even bothering with the glass. Drinking it reminded him of the three of them, breaking into Gordon's secret stash to stave off their desperation a while longer. Shit, *everything* reminded him of them in one way or another.

He pulled off his shirt, leaned back and began to pump his cock, pulling it to quick erection. He licked the middle finger of his other hand and reached under himself, lightly rimming his asshole with the tip. It felt good.

He let go of his cock long enough to grab the small tube of lubricant and squeeze some on his fingers. Cock in hand, he again touched his asshole, pushing a finger inside. He added a second finger, finding it slightly uncomfortable but at the same time, highly erotic. He'd watched Tuck do this to Jamie, opening him, readying him for a cock.

He stroked himself a while longer, finally letting the images of Tuck and Jamie, naked and in his arms, at his feet, looming over him with cocks bobbing, scroll through his mind like a silent movie.

Probably the most intense experience had been their last one, cut short by the ringing telephone. It had been incredibly hot to hold Jamie in his arms, their erect cocks colliding while Tuck entered Jamie from behind. Each thrust of Tuck's hips had forced Jamie's cock against his.

When Jamie had come on him, he hadn't been disgusted by another man's semen. On the contrary, he'd nearly come himself from Jamie's warm, wet tongue gliding over his chest and belly, licking away every drop before taking Brendan's rigid cock into his mouth. Jesus God, recalling the two of them, licking, sucking, stroking his cock and balls until he exploded in a frenzy of nearly unbearable pleasure...

Brendan dropped his cock long enough to pick up the dildo from the sofa. With shaking hands he squeezed a generous dollop of KY on its tip and touched it to his nether entrance. Holding his breath, he pressed it into himself. Much slimmer than a real cock, it slid in easily and didn't hurt at all.

He pushed it in farther, taking the length of it before resuming his cock massage. He squeezed his ass cheeks together, imagining it was Tuck inside him, taking him from behind while Jamie worked his incredible magic on his cock.

That summer night the year before whispered through his memory. Tuck leaning against him, murmuring low, so close he could have turned and kissed him. They were alone by the dying fire, exchanging sometimes funny, sometimes painful memories of childhood and teenage angst.

It had felt so good, so right, when Tuck had put his arm around Brendan's shoulder. He'd leaned into him, closing his eyes, wishing Tuck were a woman so they could fall in love. A secret part of him already knew then what he'd spent the next year denying to himself.

He'd fallen in love that night, and never fallen out. But a lifetime of self-control and rigid denial had come to bear as it always had when anything like a real emotion threatened Brendan's careful, controlled world. He'd blotted out the intensity, the utter sweetness and naked longing he'd felt for the other man, tamping it down to something more manageable and less terrifying.

Something in him had clung to his real feelings, enough so he'd managed to get Tuck onto the polar project. Then, in his usual stupid, stolid, self-denying fashion, he'd kept his feelings in check, hiding them from both Tuck and himself until it was too late.

But fate, that's what Tuck had called it and maybe he was right, fate had intervened. The blizzard and all its possible implications had stripped away his defenses, rendering himself vulnerable to Tuck and Jamie's playful sexual games. Rendering him vulnerable to his own closely held secrets, secrets he'd tried to deny since they'd come home.

The dildo was still buried between his ass cheeks. He clenched on it, almost wanting it to hurt, wanting to feel something, anything, to make him feel more connected to the two men he'd shut out of his life.

He stroked his cock, willing his mind to empty. He focused on the sensations—the hard dildo filling him, the friction of his hand moving rapidly over his shaft. Tuck and Jamie, waiting on the edges of his consciousness, slipped into his mind's eye. Tuck crouched behind him, his large, heavy cock held in his hand, its tip nudging between Brendan's cheeks. Jamie cradled Brendan's head in his lap, his thick, hard shaft pressing hotly against Brendan's lips.

He eased into the sofa, clenching his ass as Tuck slipped his hard member into him. He parted his lips to take Jamie's cock deep in his throat. "Yes," he whispered. "Yes. Please. I want it. I want you. I want you both."

His fingers flew over his cock in time to the fantasy playing out in his head. When he came, he came hard, gobs of ejaculate landing on his belly and chest, a guttural cry wrenched from his lips. He lay still for several minutes, purposely keeping the dildo clenched inside himself, holding the visions of his all-too-brief lovers in his mind.

He thought about those last intense minutes just before they got the rescue phone call, when Jamie, with Tuck's cock still buried in him from behind, had come all over him and then licked it up. He stared at his bare torso. The semen was dripping down like icing drizzled over coffeecake.

Where was Jamie, he thought with a rueful grin, when he needed him?

Where was Tuck?

He'd thrown away his first real chance at love. He'd thrown it all away because he'd been too afraid to face the truth. And now it was too late. He closed his eyes, letting tears trickle from the corners.

"What have I done?" Brendan's voice cracked in the empty room.

Chapter Fourteen

Jamie rolled over with a contented sigh. Saturday morning, the whole glorious weekend stretching ahead of them. He smiled as his eyes lighted on the black leather cuffs still dangling from the posts at the head of his bed. They'd found them at a sex boutique and though it had been his idea, Tuck had been very willing to go along. Tuck had teasingly handled the whips and crops, but Jamie had demurred, not quite ready for that level of play.

Having his wrists bound over his head, with Tuck free to do whatever he wanted, had made the sex even hotter than usual. He closed his eyes, recalling the sweet sting when Tuck had slapped his erect cock. Though Jamie didn't seek out erotic pain for its sake, he found it added an indefinable thrill to the experience.

In between the playful but sharp smacks, Tuck had pulled and stroked Jamie's shaft until the distinction between pleasure and pain had completely blurred into sheer ecstasy. He had come three times last night, each orgasm more intense than the last.

It was super sexy the way Tuck liked to take over sexually. Without Jamie ever having to say a word, Tuck had intuited his sexual nature and asserted a natural dominance that perfectly fit his groove.

He fingered the jeweled snake on the gold chain and smiled. Tuck had talked about maybe getting a tattoo himself, though he hadn't yet decided what he wanted. Having learned the hard way, Jamie had cautioned him to take his time. No names, as he'd foolishly done, because even if a relationship wasn't forever, a tattoo was.

Where was Tuck, anyway? His happiness faded when he remembered he wouldn't be seeing Tuck until Monday night. Tuck had slipped out early that morning, with the plan to drive down to Long Beach in time for his cousin's wedding and spend the weekend. He was going to drive back Monday.

When he'd first mentioned the wedding, Jamie hadn't said anything, waiting to see if he would be invited. Weddings, funerals, any sort of major family function—in Jamie's mind these were a key test of the seriousness of a relationship. Especially a gay relationship, where the partners potentially had something to lose by showing up with another man.

Since they were still relatively new as a couple, he hadn't really expected Tuck to invite him along, nor did he particularly relish the idea of spending his weekend among strangers. Still, he'd found himself inordinately pleased when Tuck asked him if he'd like to go.

"I'm sure my cousin won't mind. Her parents are rolling in dough—what's one more guest out of a list of hundreds?"

Jamie had accepted, until he recalled he was signed up for Saturday morning lab work on a critical experiment that couldn't be put off. If Tuck waited for him, they'd arrive too late.

"It's okay," Tuck had assured him. "I'm sure there'll be plenty of other boring family obligations for us to go to together."

Jamie smiled warmly at the recollection of that conversation. Tuck's easy assurance and all it implied of a real relationship between them, something lasting, something he wasn't afraid to share with the world, made Jamie feel warm and happy.

He glanced at the clock. He needed to get his ass out of bed and to the lab. After that few hours work, though, he'd have the whole weekend to himself. Maybe it was a good thing he hadn't been able to go to the wedding. Maybe some time apart would give them both perspective.

They'd spent nearly every night together in the two months they'd been home. Though Tuck had stopped bringing up Brendan, Jamie knew he was still on his mind. In fact, only two nights before, Tuck had been calling for him in his sleep. Jamie had shaken him, trying to wake him without startling him. Tuck had bolted upright, crying out, "Brendan, watch out!"

Jamie took him into his arms to soothe him. "He was being buried alive in an avalanche and I couldn't get to him. It was horrible." Tuck's voice cracked. "I miss him, Jamie. I miss him so much."

Jamie missed Brendan too, though he remained angry with him for abandoning them the way he had. He tried to understand what it must be like to be so uncomfortable with your sexuality that you denied it, not only to those who loved you, but to yourself.

Jamie was lucky in that regard. He'd never had hang-ups about being gay. Sure, there had been guys, especially in high school, who tried to pick on him for being what he was. Maybe because of the support he'd received at home from parents who never judged him and were always supportive, he'd found the confidence to stand up to the bullies. It didn't hurt that, even in high school, he was nearly six feet tall and naturally muscular and athletic.

He didn't like to fight, but he'd done it when he'd had to,

enough to establish that he wasn't someone to be messed with. The worst it got was in eleventh grade, when Randall Clements had left a note on his locker, telling him to meet him behind the bleachers. He'd gone, tired of the constant veiled threats and attempted intimidations by Clements and his two sidekicks, whose names he no longer recalled.

As he'd expected, they'd all three been there. "Oh, look, the faggot is here. Probably hopes we'll butt fuck him. Drop your pants, faggot. I've brought a broom." The asshole had actually waved a broom in his direction, his piggy eyes glittering with malice. The sidekicks sniggered. Jamie saw red.

"Touch me, motherfucker." Jamie kept his voice calm but resolute. "And you'll regret it."

Clements laughed, signaling to his pals to stand ready, real brave, three against one. Clements was bigger than he, but slower. When the bully moved to take a swing, Jamie feinted to the side and punched him hard, his knuckles cracking bone when his fist collided with Clements' jaw. As Clements reeled, Jamie punched him again, this time three hard blows to his gut, to make sure when he went down, he stayed down.

When he turned around to deal with the others, he saw them running away across the field. So much for standing by their friend. After that he'd had no more trouble, even when he brought a guy to the senior prom.

It must really suck for Brendan, he thought, to be so uncomfortable with what and who you are. Brendan, who had kissed him with such tender, sensual passion it had taken his breath away. Brendan, who had held him tight in his arms while Tuck took him from behind, his heart beating a hundred miles a minute against Jamie's own.

Yes. He missed him too.

What a shame he'd shut them off, and himself as well.

What a waste. Love was so rare, how could he turn his back in the face of it?

Maybe he would go talk some sense into him.

He rolled from the bed and went to his bureau to get some underwear for after his shower. He felt the crackle of paper and pulled out the wadded-up sheet he'd found in front of the porch the week before and, for some reason, had saved, though he hadn't let Tuck know he had it.

In Tuck's loopy, angular hand the words *Brendan Aaronson* had been scrawled over and over on the page, like a schoolgirl mooning over her first crush. At first Jamie had been hurt by this evidence of Tuck's continued longing. But he understood it. Tuck and Brendan had had something even before Jamie had come onto the scene. Watching the two of them together, it was obvious Tuck was in love with Brendan. And, deny it as he would, Brendan had been in love with Tuck as well.

Was Jamie lucky Brendan had run away? Would he have lost Tuck to Brendan if he'd stuck around? He sat again on the bed, recalling the sweet, hot intensity that had been shared between the three of them.

While he loved what was developing between Tuck and himself now, he had to admit it would be even hotter if Brendan were there to explore it with them. If only it hadn't ended so abruptly.

It was a strange thing to wish for, when back then they'd felt desperate to be rescued, but if only they'd had one more day. With one more day, they could have seduced Brendan completely, he was sure of it.

What would it have been like to watch Tuck take the virgin Brendan, while Jamie sucked his cock? Or would Brendan have been the one to press his thick, hard shaft into Jamie while Tuck lay beneath them, eagerly gobbling Jamie's cock?

Jamie shivered at the delicious possibilities. He could visualize those two built, sexy men having their way with him, filling every orifice, fucking him every which way to Sunday until he collapsed with pleasure and exhaustion.

And whatever else Brendan was or wasn't, he was easily the best looking of the three, with his sunny blond good looks, that movie star smile and those amazing green eyes that turned to gray when he was concentrating.

Jamie loved the contrast between the two men—dark, seductive Tuck with the flashing white teeth and brooding eyes, and sunny blond Brendan with that wide, engaging smile that completely disarmed Jamie each time it was bestowed upon him.

There were so many delightful variations possible when two became three. And what had been so special between the three of them was the love thrown into the mix. Yes, he would admit it. It *was* love, however fleeting, however contrived because of the desperate situation in which they found themselves.

He had fallen quickly and fallen hard for *both* men, and losing Brendan so soon after having found him had been bad enough for him. It must have been exponentially worse for Tuck, who had carried a flame for him ever since their meeting the summer before.

Damn it, what the hell was *wrong* with Brendan? He didn't have the right to just opt out. To wash his hands of them and deny his feelings. At least he could have explained himself better, instead of offering some lame cock-and-bull story about love in the trenches or whatever the fuck he had spouted to Tuck.

Maybe he *would* drive up to Seattle, talk face-to-face with Brendan and demand an answer, the real answer about why he'd run away.

He would be done in the lab by noon at the latest. After that he had nothing but time. He checked on the Internet for the best route from Carmel to Seattle. Whoa—fourteen hours. He thought a moment and shrugged. He'd make better time than that on his Harley, he was sure.

He wouldn't tell Tuck he was going. Plenty of time to tell him later.

And he wouldn't tell Brendan he was coming. Why give him a chance to prepare his excuses, or worse, to refuse to see him? No, he'd just show up on his doorstep.

What would he say when he got there?

He had no idea.

He'd play it by ear.

Hugging the motorcycle's body between his thighs, Jamie flexed his leather-gloved hands, trying to keep them from cramping. He'd been gripping the bars for hours, flying up the highway toward Seattle, the wind in his face, the sun beating down.

With the sun's setting, the air had turned cool, too cool for a thin leather jacket and jeans. Not to mention, after seven hours on the bike, every muscle in Jamie's body screamed for a break.

What had he been thinking? No way was he going to reach Brendan's at a decent hour. While he'd definitely made good time, especially once he'd made it onto I-5 North, he was still a good four-hundred-fifty miles away from Seattle. Better to find a cheap motel, get some rest and head out first thing.

Thus he found himself in the parking lot of a stucco two-story building painted a bright flamingo pink with a neon sign advertising vacancies in glowing orange. He parked his bike and made his way into the brightly lit lobby. He asked for a room for the night, thinking he'd grab something to eat at the diner located next door.

"You just passing through?" The woman behind the counter was young, maybe early twenties, with lank blonde hair and too much makeup on a pretty if uninteresting face.

"Yeah. Trip's taking a little longer than I was hoping."

"That your motorcycle out there?" She handed him the keycard to his room, her fingers brushing his as she fixed him with a limpid gaze. "I just *love* motorcycles. They're just so...masculine. I don't know, *virile*. You know what I mean?"

Jamie withdrew his hand from beneath hers and smiled, shaking his head. "Yeah. I know what you mean." He pocketed the key and his wallet and turned from the counter, eager to nip whatever ideas the girl was getting in the bud. "Well, have a good night."

"I get off my shift in fifteen minutes. Maybe you could take me for a ride. We could go out for a drink or something." She blinked rapidly at him in a way he knew was meant to be seductive and pressed her arms against the sides of her small breasts in an effort to create cleavage.

He was used to women hitting on him, and usually he handled himself with more finesse, but he was hungry and too bone-weary to behave with his usual tact. "I would, but my boyfriend is super jealous and if he found out, he'd beat the crap out of me," Jamie lied, suppressing a grin. "So I'll have to pass, sorry."

The girl's eyes widened, her mouth falling open as she took in the implication of his words. Her arms fell to her sides and she stepped back from the counter as if he'd struck her. "I—I see," she stammered. "Well, have a good night and welcome to Medford."

The room wasn't bad. At least it was clean. He sat on the slippery polyester bedspread and pulled out his cell phone, punching in the speed dial for Tuck. It went to voice mail, Tuck's low sexy voice suggesting he leave a message. He was probably at the reception by now, toasting the happiness of his cousin.

"Hey, Tuck. Jamie here. Just wanted to say good night. Let you know I'm thinking about you. No need to call back. We'll connect in the morning. Love you."

Love you. He'd never actually said the complete sentence—I love you. Nor had Tuck. Yet they ended phone conversations with those two words, a sort of substitute for goodbye.

I do love him, though. Next time I see him face-to-face, I'm going to tell him so.

His tummy rumbled, reminding him he hadn't eaten since the beef jerky he'd bought at the gas station some four hours before. After washing his face and running his fingers through his hair, he left the motel room, heading toward the diner and a meal for one.

Jamie fumbled with his cell phone. "Yeah?"

"Jamie? Hey, were you sleeping? I'm sorry. I had left my cell phone back in the room so I missed your call earlier."

"Tuck. Hey. That's okay. What time is it?" Jamie sat up against the uncomfortable headboard in his motel room. It was dark outside, the orange glow of the neon sign from outside his window blinking against one wall.

"It's midnight. I'm sorry. I shouldn't have called so late. I just missed you."

"Yeah?" Jamie adjusted the pillows beneath his head and slid back down. "Cool. Was the wedding fun?"

"Fun?" Tuck laughed. "No, it was fucking endless. The groom is a Greek Orthodox something or other and the service lasted over two hours. I thought I was going to keel over from the boredom. I kept looking around at all the people, most of whom had the same glazed expression. I imagined the whole congregation, on cue, all slumping over to one side and sliding down onto the floor."

Jamie offered a rueful grin. "I wish I could have been there to prop you up. Was the reception good at least?"

"Yeah. It was great. The food was fantastic, the bar was open and there were even a few hotties I had my eye on."

"Male or female?" Despite their light tones, Jamie couldn't help feeling a jolt of jealousy.

"Both. That's the advantage of playing both sides of the fence." Tuck laughed. "Hey, I'm just teasing you, babe. No one there held a candle to you, I promise."

"So you're settled for the night? How's your room?"

"Oh, it's fine. Sophie reserved three entire floors of the hotel for guests and got a great rate. I just wish you were here with me. Or better yet, that I was back in your cozy cottage by the sea."

Jamie didn't respond right away. He toyed with the idea of telling Tuck he was actually somewhere in Oregon, on his way to see Brendan. But he didn't want Tuck to try to talk him out of it, so he remained silent. He would do this on his own. Instead he said, "So, you miss me, huh?"

"I do. I've been thinking. When I get back, I'm going to try out those nipple clamps I've been threatening you with. What do you think of that?"

Jamie shivered and touched his chest, his nipples perking to attention. Tuck had a knack of saying things that gave him an instant erection. "Jesus, Tuck. I was asleep and now look what you've done to me. I'm harder than a rock." He lifted the sheet, staring down at his erection.

"I wish I could look. Save that cock for me, okay? I miss it. I miss you."

"I miss you too, Tuck. A lot." It was true. "Tuck, I..." Again he almost confided where he was and what he was doing. Was he making a mistake? Should he let sleeping dogs lie, let Brendan fade away from their lives? Well, whatever he was doing, there was no turning back now. He was more than halfway there. He would see this thing through, however it played out.

"Yeah?"

"Nothing. Love you."

"Love you."

Chapter Fifteen

Brendan squinted in the early morning light slanting into the bedroom window. He was naked, on his stomach, the covers twisted around his legs, his arm hanging over the side of the bed.

The doorbell was ringing, that's what that sound was that had awoken him. It was followed a moment later by a loud knocking. Brendan looked at the clock by his bed. It was seven o'clock on a Sunday morning, for crying out loud. Who in God's name was banging on his door at this hour?

He pulled himself up and grabbed the jeans he'd dropped on the floor beside the bed the night before, not bothering with underwear. As he weaved unsteadily toward the living room, his mind raced over what emergency might be awaiting him at his front door.

His parents had retired to Arizona and both his sisters lived in Southern California. If something had happened to any of them, he'd be getting a phone call, not a personal summons via a fist on the door. If something was wrong at the lab, again, he would have been called. So who the hell was out there? Surely not Lynn. Her style was more subtle, icy rage, not banging and bell ringing.

Brendan had spent a second lonely night experimenting with the dildo and drinking himself numb. His head was aching and he didn't feel ready to face whatever was on the other side of that door.

He peered out the peephole. He froze, his heart constricting, his breath catching. Jamie Hunter stood there, real as life. He was wearing a soft brown leather jacket over a white T-shirt, a helmet cradled beneath his arm. His face was sunburned, making his blue eyes even more brilliant than usual. He jabbed the bell several times in succession and lifted his hand to rap at the door. Brendan pulled it open.

Jamie dropped his hand and took a step back, as if surprised someone had actually opened the door at last. "Brendan. Hi."

"Jamie." Brendan pulled the door open and stepped back. "It's seven in the morning. Is everything okay?" The sudden horrible realization everything might not be okay hit Brendan like a ton of bricks. He nearly reeled with the thought. "Oh my God," he breathed. "Tuck...?"

"Tuck's fine." Jamie's tone was brusque. He moved past him into the room. "He doesn't know I'm here."

Brendan realized too late he'd left the bottle of scotch and empty glass on the coffee table, evidence of his lonely night. Thank God at least he'd removed the dildo to the bathroom sink and thrown out the packaging it had come in.

"You, uh, you drove here? All the way from Monterey?"

"I came on my bike, yeah. Stopped in Oregon overnight. I couldn't sleep so I headed out this morning again around two."

Brendan still didn't get it. He wasn't fully awake, for one thing, his head still fogged with sleep and the aftereffects of too much booze the night before. Jamie turned to him, his hands on his hips, his tone at once apologetic and defensive. "Look, I'm sorry I just came bursting in here at this hour. I had to see you. I couldn't wait another second."

"Me? You had to see me?"

"Yeah. We have some stuff we need to talk about. That and I—I missed you." He moved closer. Brendan stepped back and Jamie scowled.

Silently Brendan cursed himself. Aloud he said, "Uh, you want some coffee or something? I'm not really awake yet."

"Sure. Yeah. That'd be good." Jamie followed him into the kitchen, where Brendan busied himself with the coffeemaker while he tried to figure out what the hell was going on.

He set mugs, sugar and cream on the table and gestured for Jamie to sit. "I just need to use the bathroom and get dressed. Help yourself to the coffee when it's done. I'll be right out."

He hurried to his bedroom, still not completely processing who was in the other room. Jamie Hunter. *Jamie.* Over the last two nights he'd shed tears, trying to come to terms with the fact he'd never see this sexy, handsome guy again, forcing himself to admit he'd closed the doors on something amazing between the three of them because of his own cowardice.

Brendan stared in horror at the dildo he'd left soaking in the bathroom sink the night before. What if Jamie had asked to use the bathroom? Hurriedly he rinsed it off and shoved it into the back of the drawer beneath the counter.

A dawning sense of hope edged over the horizon of his consciousness. Jamie Hunter wasn't a thousand miles away with the man Brendan couldn't forget. He was sitting in Brendan's kitchen sipping coffee. Life didn't often come with a second chance. Was that what this was? *Don't jump to conclusions,* Brendan admonished himself as he washed his face and brushed his teeth. *He might only be here to tell you in person what an asshole you are.*

Brendan recalled the pain in Tuck's voice after he had

171

delivered his pompous, stupid sermon about facing reality and letting go of fantasies. No doubt Tuck had relayed the conversation, while taking comfort in Jamie's welcoming arms. Maybe Jamie was only here to settle the score.

He pulled on a fresh shirt and headed back to the kitchen, ready to face his just desserts. Jamie had poured himself a mug of coffee and was sipping it. Brendan entered the room and helped himself to the coffee. He sat across from Jamie and tried to smile. No matter what dire message Jamie had come to deliver, it was *so* good to see him again.

It was odd to see him out of context. The whole bizarre experience had been preserved in his mind like reels of old film he'd take out and watch again and again. On one level, Jamie only existed as a memory, frozen in time against a backdrop of snow and ice.

What an amazing couple of days they'd had. What a sexy, generous lover Jamie had been. He looked so good, even better than memory had served. His light brown hair was shiny, falling in shaggy waves over his eyes and down the back of his neck. His mouth was sensuously curved, the very mouth that had sucked Brendan's cock, accepted his kisses, whispered sexy, dangerous things that even now Brendan blushed to recall...

He watched Jamie sipping his coffee, glad Jamie couldn't see into his head. He had an urge to drop to his knees at Jamie's feet and wrap his arms around his legs, while begging forgiveness for being such an ass.

Jamie would laugh in his face. Jamie had probably been glad he'd excused himself from the ménage, leaving Tuck all to himself. But if that was true, what was he doing here?

"It's good to see you, Jamie. Are you, uh...are you and Tuck together?" *Are you lovers? Do you ever think of me while you're fucking each other?*

"Yeah. Two out of three." He was surprised by the bitterness in Jamie's voice.

So they were together. Of course they were. Lovers, with Brendan nothing more than a memory. Then he replayed Jamie's words. Two out of three. Was he the third? Brendan's heart lurched. God he missed them, missed Tuck, missed the closeness, the heat, the passion, the raw, aching sweetness.

He hoped his voice would remain steady when he spoke. "How's Tuck?"

Jamie's smile was paper thin. "Tuck is fine. No thanks to you."

Brendan felt himself flushing. He looked away.

"You broke his heart, Brendan. It's as simple as that."

As simple as that.

Anger rose in Brendan's gut like corrosive acid. The anger was easier to handle than the sorrow and the shame. He clung to it, letting its poison pervade his psyche. Who the fuck was this little prick to barge into his home at the crack of dawn and accuse him of something like that? Why wasn't Tuck speaking for himself? If his heart was so broken, why hadn't he ever called again? Didn't he understand how difficult this was for a straight guy to come to grips with?

"I *what*? I got news for you, Jamie. You can't break someone's heart unless they're in love. Correct me if I'm wrong, but you just admitted the two of you are lovers. How the fuck am I supposed to compete with that? You live in the same town, work in the same damn building, see each other every day. I'm up here, a thousand miles away, the *curious* one, the anomaly, the straight guy it was a challenge to seduce and then forget—"

"How *dare* you." Jamie's voice cut across Brendan's rant. "Nobody's forgotten you, Brendan. Shit, if we could forget you, would I be here? Nobody seduced you—not in the way you're

173

implying. You were ready, willing and able. You were as into us as we were into you. Then the rescue 'copter shows up and you do a one-eighty. Suddenly the open, tolerant, bi-curious guy becomes Mr. Straight Asshole, callously chocking up whatever had happened between us three as some kind of aberrant homosexual fling, the stuff of desperate men facing war or whatever the fuck you dribbled into Tuck's ear like liquid shit."

Brendan opened his mouth to protest, outrage and bitter shame fighting a duel inside him, the slashing pain of it rendering him mute.

Jamie wasn't done. "Yeah, you're right. You have to be in love to have your heart broken. He's in love with you, asshole. He's been in love with you since before Antarctica. If you weren't so busy shoving your cowardly head up your ass to keep from admitting your real feelings, you'd know that. Christ, Brendan. You'd know how we both felt. How I feel..."

Jamie's voice cracked, his handsome face a mask of pain. He stood and blew out a deep breath. "Jesus. This isn't what I'd planned. I don't know what I was planning, really. I didn't get that far in my head. I'm sorry. I have no right to talk to you like this. You made your position abundantly clear on the phone. I don't know what I was thinking. I wasn't thinking at all, I guess."

"Jamie." Brendan tried to speak but a lump had formed in his throat. If he said another word he would start crying.

"No." Jamie held up his hand. "Look, go back to bed." He gave a small, bitter laugh. "I'm such a jerk. Here I kept advising Tuck to let it go, then the minute he's out of town I hop on my bike and ride up here, like it's going to make a difference, like any of this matters to you." He turned to go.

"No. Please. Jamie, don't go."

It was too late. Jamie strode out of the kitchen. Brendan

sat, rooted to his chair for several horrible seconds. Finally he found the wherewithal to move and leaped up, running into the living room in time to hear the door slam.

Sprinting, he raced to the door and flung it open. "Jamie! Jamie, don't go. You can't go. Please. Come back. I need you. Please."

Jamie had his helmet on and was kicking at the stand of his motorcycle. Brendan watched helplessly. When Jamie climbed onto the bike, Brendan sank to the ground, hiding his head in his hands. His heart split with pain for all that he'd done and all that he'd lost.

If the engine hadn't stalled, Jamie wouldn't have known Brendan followed him. He wouldn't have turned back to see him crumpled at his doorway, his head bowed, his shoulders shaking.

Jamie's heart contracted with pity. He hadn't meant to lash out like that. He hadn't even realized he was carrying so much anger. He climbed off his bike, not willing to leave Brendan alone and crying. He'd never meant to make the man weep. The trembling rage he'd felt when he tore out of there had evaporated in the face of Brendan's tears.

He thought back to that day in Antarctica, when it had been Jamie's turn to break down. Brendan had comforted him, just holding him in his arms, no questions asked. He'd felt safe then, in an unsafe world. Brendan had protected him and accepted him without judgment.

Jamie climbed off his bike and removed his helmet. He returned to Brendan. "Hey. Hey, Brendan. It's okay. Come on. I'm sorry."

Brendan didn't respond. Jamie crouched beside him. He touched Brendan's shoulder but Brendan shook him off. He raised a tear-streaked face. "Sorry...I didn't mean...don't want you to see me like this...please...just go..."

Jamie stayed where he was. Brendan got to his feet and stumbled back into his house, trying to push the door closed. Jamie stood and blocked the door with his shoulder. Brendan gave up, retreating into the room.

Jamie followed him to the couch. He sat beside Brendan and put a hand on his shoulder. Brendan continued to cry, hiding his face in one hand. Feeling helpless, Jamie looked around the room. He spied a box of tissues on a side table and hurried to retrieve it.

He pulled three tissues from the box and set them on Brendan's lap. Brendan, still without looking at Jamie, grabbed them and wiped his eyes and nose. He was still crying, but more quietly now. Jamie put his hand on Brendan's thigh, half expecting him to push it away.

Instead Brendan put his own hand over Jamie's and looked at him, smiling crookedly between his tears. "Man. I'm really sorry. You must think I'm such a... I don't usually..." He shrugged helplessly.

"Don't. Don't apologize for crying. I'm sorry I was such a shit. I didn't really plan on coming all this way just to tell you what an ass you were."

"Well, you were right. Everything you said was true. I accepted the love you both offered me and then I turned around and trivialized and denied it because I was scared."

"I know." Jamie stroked Brendan's wet cheek. "But me barreling in and bludgeoning you over the head with it wasn't exactly the coolest thing I've ever done. I'm sorry. I can be a real horse's ass myself sometimes."

"Thanks for coming back, Jamie." Brendan shook his head. "Thanks for coming all the way up here to see me."

"Even if what I had to say wasn't what you wanted to hear, huh?"

"Yeah, but maybe it's what I needed to hear. Though it might surprise you to know it's nothing I haven't been telling myself. I just figured it was too late. I'd already blown it with you guys. You had moved on and I was trying like hell to figure out how to move on myself."

He wiped his face with a soggy tissue. Jamie held out the box. "You want to wash your face or something?"

"Yeah." Brendan stood and drew in a long, shuddering breath. "Man. I haven't cried like that since I was eight years old. I didn't even know I knew how."

Jamie smiled. He wanted to draw Brendan down into his arms and just hold him, but he sensed Brendan was trying to recover himself and being held was maybe the last thing he wanted. So instead Jamie suggested, "Maybe we should go get breakfast or something. Any good diners around here?"

Brendan looked gratefully at him. "Yeah. Sure. That's a great idea. Just sit tight, I'll be right back."

Jamie leaned back against the sofa with a sigh. Tuck wouldn't have made Brendan cry. He would have handled things so much better.

He looked around the room while he waited. It was a masculine room, with dark leather furniture, two walls lined with bookshelves, another with a large old wooden desk on which sat a flat-screen monitor and piles of papers and research texts. The floors were hardwood, stained a rich reddish brown. A large bay window faced the tree-lined street.

To keep himself occupied, Jamie got up and moved toward one of the bookshelves. Most of the books were nonfiction, large tomes on various esoteric scientific subjects. One shelf was filled with paperback mysteries and science-fiction novels, clearly much read.

There were several books in French. Jamie picked one up, titled *Rendez-vous avec la mort* and saw it was by Agatha Christie, a translation. He flipped through the pages, which might as well have been in Aramaic as far as he was concerned, and recalled Brendan's story about losing his virginity to his French tutor.

They knew so little about each other, he realized. They'd worked side by side for six weeks, yet it was only in those last few days they'd connected. Could the feelings he felt for Brendan really be love? If not love, the precursor to it? He was in love with Tuck, of that he was certain. Yet he'd been drawn to Brendan, and Brendan's rejection, which he was sure was based purely on fear, hadn't lessened his desire.

Yes, the anger was still there for the way Brendan had shut them out, but it had lost its sting. He was making his peace with Brendan. That didn't mean, he knew, that Brendan was necessarily going to come running back to them. It was possible he just didn't have it in him. His curiosity, if that's what they wanted to call it, might only run so deep. As much as Tuck and Jamie wanted Brendan, maybe he just wasn't capable of any kind of sustained relationship with other men.

Nevertheless, he was glad he had come to Seattle, and even gladder he had stayed. He would have remained angry with Brendan, and had added anger at himself for his abrupt, immature departure if he'd left after his melodramatic speech.

Well, Brendan had given him a second chance. They would start over, and this time Jamie would give Brendan a chance to talk. He would listen and try to understand.

Brendan returned to the living room. His eyes were still red but his hair was combed and he'd added a dark blue work shirt over his light blue T-shirt. He smiled at Jamie. "Found my books, huh? I can't ever get rid of a book, even if it's terrible."

"Can you actually read these? The stuff in French?" Jamie waved the book he was holding toward Brendan.

"Yeah. If I have a dictionary with me. It's the slang that kills you, though. Christie is easier—not so much slang. Modern books though, forget it. You really need to live in a place to pick up their slang. I've been to France, but never for longer than a month at a time."

Jamie, who had never been out of the States, other than their fateful trip to Antarctica, was impressed. "I'd like to travel someday. I'd like to go to the Himalayas and Amsterdam. And Paris, of course."

"Of course." Brendan grinned. "It really is the most romantic city in the world. I'd love to go back." He smiled dreamily, as if recalling some romantic memory.

Jamie wanted to take him into his arms, to kiss his swollen eyelids, to stroke his cheek and hold him, to say again how sorry he was for making him cry. He took a step toward him, licking his lips in anticipation of their kiss.

Brendan suddenly snapped out of his reverie and turned away, his voice strident. "Let's go get something to eat. I'm starving."

Jamie stopped in his tracks. The moment was lost. He put the book back onto the shelf, wondering if their timing would always be off.

Chapter Sixteen

"I didn't realize how hungry I was." Jamie took another bite of French toast. He dragged a piece of sausage through the syrup and ate that as well. "This is delicious."

"Yeah." Brendan nodded. "I haven't been here for a while." He chewed a bite of his blueberry blintz. He could hardly believe it was really Jamie sitting across from him right there in Seattle, instead of consigned forever to bittersweet memory.

Jamie thanked the waitress when she topped off his coffee. He turned back to Brendan. "So you were, like, engaged to a woman? And you've always only dated women?" They had been talking in general about sexual orientation—gay versus straight, with Jamie holding forth about his theory that no one was purely one thing or the other.

"Yeah," Brendan admitted. "Tuck and you were my first, um, real experience."

"So never before? No teenage experimentation? No crush on an athlete, something like that?"

"Well, yeah. I mean, I guess I've always had crushes, to use your phrase, on guys. I mean, I didn't define it like that. I admired them. I found them attractive, you know, but I didn't think of it as sexual precisely."

"Precisely? So just sort of?" Jamie grinned and Brendan felt himself blushing. Jamie continued his relentless questioning.

"So when you were a kid, there wasn't that one boy in ninth grade who slipped into your fantasies while you were jerking off under the covers or in the shower? That one guy in college who, after a few beers too many, *accidentally* groped you instead of his girlfriend?" Jamie smirked.

Brendan felt his face heat. Jesus, had he left some kind of window open inside his head for Jamie to peer into and make fun of? Zach Hickman. He hadn't thought about Zach in years.

It wasn't ninth grade, but tenth. They were both on the track team. Zach had long dark hair he wore loose. His features were almost feminine—a cupid's bow of a mouth and large dark eyes. In fact, Brendan used to tell himself he was only attracted to him because of his feminine traits, in those moments he admitted to himself he was attracted at all.

Zach had just turned sixteen, while Brendan was still fifteen. He was spending the night at Zach's, and they were celebrating Zach's birthday with a fifth of blackberry brandy Zach had convinced his older brother to buy for them.

It was a warm, sticky summer night. They were lying on the bottom bunk in Zach's bedroom in just their gym shorts, listening to music, getting drunk and talking about nothing much. The light was out and it was late.

Brendan fell asleep at one point and when he woke, Zach was draped over him, his hand on Brendan's crotch, his eyes closed. What the hell was going on? Brendan realized he had a full erection and his heart began to pound. He lay still, wondering what to do, both frightened and aroused by Zach's proximity and touch. He didn't dare to move for a full minute. Zach seemed to be asleep, but the limp weight of his hand was driving Brendan crazy.

He finally got up the nerve to move his hips a little and Zach's hand shifted, his fingers brushing Brendan's cock through the thin cotton of his shorts. At the same time, he could feel Zach's erection press against him.

They began a silent, unacknowledged sexual dance, with Zach's fingers responding with gentle but insistent pressure each time Brendan moved his hips, accompanied by the subtle press of his hard shaft against Brendan's side.

Brendan kept his eyes closed and tried to keep his breathing regular and even, mimicking Zach's pretense of being asleep. They continued the charade until each boy, within seconds of one another, ejaculated in their underwear.

Zach rolled away from Brendan, who lay still, his heart pounding, for a good ten minutes before daring to move. Zach appeared to be asleep. Brendan crept out of bed and cleaned himself up as best he could in the bathroom.

When he returned, Zach was still in the same position, on his side, his face to the wall. Brendan climbed into the top bunk, half-wondering if he'd dreamt the whole thing.

Things seemed to change between them after that. Zach avoided Brendan, which hurt his feelings and confused him. Brendan wanted to bring up what had happened, to ask Zach what he thought, but he never dared. Zach never said a word. After a while it was as if it had never been, except that the easy friendship they'd shared since childhood was never regained.

"Oh my God," Jamie crowed. "There was something. I can see it in your face. Come on. Tell me about him. Did anything happen, or was it just teenage longing confined to the pages of your secret diary?"

Embarrassment made Brendan terse. "What is this, your mission in Seattle? To delve into my past to find out why I'm so fucked up now and then make fun of it?"

The smile fell away from Jamie's face. "No. I'm sorry, Bren. I was being flip. That's what I do, you know? I make fun of stuff to keep it light." He reached across the table and touched Brendan's hand. "I'm sorry. I actually really want to know. I want to understand how someone can go through their life without ever connecting to such a basic part of themselves.

"What we shared, what we experienced during the blizzard—it was more than just three horny, scared guys trying to distract themselves from their situation. It was definitely more for Tuck and for me, but I think it was more for you too. I know it was.

"That's why I came to see you, Brendan. I need to understand. Even if nothing more comes of this than that, I have to know who you are—who the guy is who fell into our hearts in so short a time and then just...disappeared."

Brendan said nothing. Jamie continued. "Was what we shared just an aberration in your mind? Deviant behavior engaged in to stave off the fear of death? Something to be shoved under the rug with the rest of your unacceptable experiences and feelings once you made it safely home? Don't you owe it to us to at least explain yourself?"

Brendan hung his head, tears again pushing behind his eyes. Damn it, he was most certainly not going to cry in a restaurant. He looked up into Jamie's face. "I don't know what I owe to whom. I don't know what I feel. Maybe that's the real issue for me. I've never known how to connect with my feelings. How to accept them without analyzing the crap out of them and judging myself and trying to push everything into neat, acceptable slots like vials in a science lab, each in its proper place."

Again the tears rose, hot and heavy behind his eyes. Brendan pressed his fingers to his eyelids.

"Hey, I'm sorry." Jamie's voice was kind. "I don't want to upset you again. That's not my intention. I really want to understand. You done eating? Maybe we could go back to your place and talk some more. Would that be okay?"

Brendan dropped his hands and smiled at Jamie. "Why do I feel like the kid here?"

"Probably just my superior intellect. I have that effect on people. Don't feel bad." Jamie laughed and Brendan laughed with him. He hadn't laughed in a long time. It felt good.

"You look beat." They had returned to Brendan's place and were seated, facing one another, on the sofa.

Jamie yawned. His eyes felt like they were full of sand. "I am. I only slept a few hours last night. I was too keyed up, I guess. I probably should sleep some before I head back." The thought of the twelve or thirteen hour motorcycle ride down to Monterey did not appeal.

"When do you have to go? I don't want you to go."

Jamie smiled. "I don't want to go either, but I'm supposed to be at work tomorrow." He looked at his watch. "Even if I left now and rode straight through, I wouldn't make it home till eleven. And I really can't sit on that damn cycle for more than four hours without some kind of break, so it'll be more like one a.m."

"Well, that's just crazy. You can't possibly do that, especially on no sleep. You're just going to have to call in sick. You don't want to risk your life for a damn job, do you?"

"No. But I've only been there a year, you know. I'm still the new kid on the block."

"Well, I'm sure they'll forgive you for calling in sick one time. I want you to stay a while longer. Please?"

"How can I resist you?" Jamie leaned toward Brendan, expecting at least a kiss.

Instead Brendan stood, offering something even better. "Let's lie down so you can rest. We can continue our conversation from the diner. You know, the one where I shed light on why I'm such a repressed fuckup." He laughed lightly, though Jamie saw the pain in his eyes. "I'm sure I'll bore you sufficiently that you'll be asleep in no time."

Jamie followed Brendan into the bedroom, his cock nudging in his jeans even though Brendan's offer was platonic. He *was* incredibly tired, his eyelids drooping and his concentration wandering, despite his best efforts to remain alert.

The bed felt wonderful, especially after the lumpy, uncomfortable motel mattress and the hours hunched over his cycle. He stretched and sighed with contentment. "I could get used to this."

Brendan lay down beside him. They were both fully clothed. Jamie sensed Brendan wanted to talk some more. He'd begun to talk again while driving back from the diner, speculating aloud about why he never quite connected in the serious relationships he'd had during his life. He hadn't been especially surprised to hear Brendan had been involved with a woman since their return from Antarctica. He guessed he was more surprised that Brendan had ended it. Hearing this gave him his first real spark of hope. But he needed to hear more, to understand more about the nature of their relationship and the breakup. How did Brendan define himself now? Was he still merely curious, or was he finally ready to admit to something more?

To give him an opening, Jamie offered, "You were talking about Lynn. About her accusation that you would never be ready for a committed relationship. Do you think that's true, or do you think you've just been looking in the wrong place."

"You know, if you'd shown up one week earlier, I might have thought she was right—that I was just a fucked-up, closed-off asshole who was never going to connect with anyone on a meaningful level. I'd blown it with every other woman I'd ever been involved with. It honestly never occurred to me I was looking in the wrong place, as you put it. Not till..."

"Not till..." Jamie prompted.

"Till I met Tuck last year. But even then, even then I denied it to myself. I was scared of my own intense reaction to him. To his physical presence, to his sensuality. Even when I finagled his invitation to the research team, I managed to convince myself we were just friends."

"But you loved him already, didn't you?" Jamie whispered the words, not sure himself how they made him feel. Would he always be jealous of the special bond Brendan and Tuck had forged before he ever came on the scene?

"Yeah." The word was ripe with emotion, conveying longing and loss, coupled with a kind of awe.

Jamie had been lying on his back, Brendan likewise beside him. He rolled toward Brendan now, aware what a monumental admission this was for him. "He loves you too, you know. I wasn't lying before."

Brendan turned toward him, his expression at once hopeful and fearful. "He told you that?"

"Yeah. Not in so many words, but yeah. Wanna see something?" Jamie reached into his back pocket and withdrew his wallet. He opened it and extracted the wrinkled, folded piece of paper he'd put there the day before. He handed it to Brendan.

Brendan opened the paper and scanned it. He looked at Jamie with a question on his face.

"Tuck did that. Just like in junior high. Your name, over and over. He doesn't know I found it. I'd say it's proof you're on his mind, wouldn't you agree?"

Brendan stared at the crumpled page, smoothing it against his leg. He was smiling, that open, sunny smile that turned him from merely handsome to heart-stoppingly gorgeous. "Can I...uh, can I have this?"

Jamie laughed. "Sure. Keep it. I guess I brought it for you."

Brendan carefully folded the paper until it was a small, neat square. He pushed it into his back pocket and reached for Jamie.

Jamie rolled into his arms and Brendan held him tight. It felt good. As much as he loved Tuck, it felt good to reconnect with Brendan. "Hey," he murmured against Brendan's neck. "I missed you. Not just Tuck. Me. I've missed you so much."

Brendan held him tighter. "Me too. Me too, Jamie. More than you'll ever know."

Jamie relaxed for the first time since he'd made the rash decision to come to Seattle. There was hope—real hope—flaring up inside him like a warm, engulfing flame. He closed his eyes, fatigue rolling over him, dragging him, despite his best efforts, into a much-needed sleep. Giving in, he closed his eyes and slipped away.

Jamie drifted in and out of a languorous sleep. Tuck's hands felt wonderful, massaging his back, strong fingers kneading into muscle. Tuck's hands moved lower, slipping into Jamie's jeans. He cupped Jamie's ass cheeks. Jamie sighed with pleasure and snuggled against Tuck's warm, bare chest. The curling chest hair was soft against his cheek and he rubbed it like it was a baby's blanket.

Tuck doesn't have chest hair.

187

Jamie opened his eyes, suddenly recalling where he was and who he was with. Those were Brendan's hands pulling him close. Brendan's cock pressing hard against him. He nuzzled again against Brendan's chest and reached down, finding the zipper on Brendan's jeans.

Brendan shifted back, allowing him to open them. He in turn reached for Jamie's fly. Without speaking, they pushed down denim, pushed up cotton, tugged and shifted until they both lay naked, on their sides facing one another.

The bedroom was drenched in a warm, butterscotch light from the sun shining through closed blinds. "How long was I sleeping?"

"About an hour." Brendan smiled shyly at Jamie. "I didn't mean to wake you." He fingered the pendant at Jamie's throat. "What's this? Oh, it's a snake. Like your tattoo."

"Yeah. Tuck got it for me for my birthday."

Brendan fingered the jeweled snake. "It's beautiful." Jamie saw the pain in his eyes. He understood the loss Brendan must feel from his self-imposed exile. They had moved on without him and he knew it.

To distract Brendan as much as anything, Jamie wrapped his hand around Brendan's cock, which had remained hard despite his sorrow. Brendan drew in his breath and ducked his head. After a moment he in turn curled his fingers around Jamie's shaft.

They massaged one another, matching strokes, sighing their mutual pleasure. After several minutes, Jamie leaned his face close to Brendan's ear. "I want to taste you."

"Jamie." Brendan bit his lip, his eyes closed, his cheeks tinting. Jamie found himself moved by the older man's shyness but obvious desire. He let go of Brendan's cock and twisted himself on the bed until he was upside down, his mouth poised at Brendan's groin, his own cock near Brendan's face.

He licked a ring around the crown before taking the hard, hot shaft between his lips. Brendan moaned his approval. Jamie licked his way down until his nose met the soft down of Brendan's pubic hair.

"Whatever you're doing, it's fucking amazing." Brendan groaned, pressing his face against Jamie's stomach, so far ignoring his erect cock. Jamie focused on pleasing Brendan, on drawing those sexy moans from his lips. He milked the shaft with his throat muscles until Brendan was panting, his hips swiveling.

Jamie pulled back from Brendan's cock long enough to say, "Take me in your mouth." It wasn't a request. He needed to feel Brendan's tongue and lips on his cock. Brendan obeyed, licking tentatively over the head and then taking the shaft partway into his mouth. He gripped the base of the shaft and drew his hand up to meet his lips.

"Yes, yes. That's it." Jamie lowered himself again, taking Brendan's length as he went. Brendan kept his lips around Jamie's cock. Jamie began to thrust. Brendan gagged but held on, which turned Jamie on. While he felt completely submissive with Tuck, something about the novice Brendan brought out a certain dominance in him.

Reaching down, he grabbed Brendan's head, holding him in position as he guided his shaft deeper into Brendan's mouth. At the same time, he kept Brendan's cock deep in his throat, pulling back only long enough to catch a breath before impaling himself once again.

Spasms shuddered through Brendan's body. Jamie could feel them in his own body, as if the two of them were directly connected by some kind of erotic kinetic force. When Brendan began to ejaculate, Jamie's body followed his lead. He held

Brendan's head, not permitting him to pull back while he thrust and spurt into his captive mouth.

Only when he was completely spent did he release Brendan's head, allowing him to fall back against the mattress. He, too, released Brendan's cock and scooted back around so they were again face-to-face.

A trickle of semen glistened at the corner of Brendan's mouth. Jamie leaned forward and licked it away.

Brendan's eyes were pure gray in the suffused light of the room. "Whoa." Brendan shook his head.

"Whoa?"

"Yeah. As in, whoa, that was amazing."

Jamie smiled. "I wasn't too rough? Making you swallow?"

"That was pretty intense. I'm not used to being out of control like that. Maybe it's what I need, though."

"Yeah. I understand." He did understand, completely. Brendan, even more so than himself, was used to controlling every aspect of his world. He liked to break things down in a lab, solve riddles, answer questions and then write it all up in neat, comprehensive reports.

Sex wasn't like that. It could be messy, even dangerous. There was a risk when you put yourself out there. He'd taken a risk coming to Brendan. Brendan had taken a risk in accepting him.

All at once Jamie understood he'd done the right thing by coming alone. If Tuck had come it would have been about him, about him and Brendan. Jamie would have been on the sidelines, no matter how much the other two tried to include him.

He recognized he hadn't ridden all this way just to confront Brendan and force him to own up to his behavior. He'd come for himself. To prove something to himself. Because what he'd just shared with Brendan had nothing to do with Tuck.

Yes, Tuck was still there, hovering in each of their hearts, but by meeting Brendan alone, by confronting him on his own terms, Jamie had learned something important. He wasn't just Tuck's consolation prize, or someone Brendan had tolerated during the blizzard in order to be near the true object of his desire.

No, in coming here alone Jamie had proven to himself he was part of the three, as important in their romantic triangle as either of the other two. The realization gave him a new sense of power and release. Jealousy no longer had a place in his heart.

He reached for Brendan, drawing him into a tight embrace. "Thank you," he whispered. "Thanks for letting me in on my own terms. Thanks for taking the chance."

"Thanks for giving me the chance."

Chapter Seventeen

"Hey, Tuck, what brings you to the fourth floor? Trying to steal my latest breakthrough?" Paul Holmes, who ran the lab where Jamie conducted most of his research, slapped Tuck on the back with a guffaw. He and Tuck engaged in a good-natured rivalry between labs, though Tuck suspected Paul took the competition for publishable results far more seriously than he did, and that his glib bonhomie was less than sincere.

Though he'd told Jamie he wouldn't be home until late Monday evening, in fact he had left very early that morning, hoping to surprise Jamie in the lab and take him to lunch. He'd missed him to distraction over the seemingly endless weekend. He'd almost left the night before, and would have except for various family events he felt obligated to attend.

"I was here to see Jamie Hunter. Is he around?"

Paul assumed a mock scowl. "Don't tell me he's the mole who's been leaking our State secrets to the enemy." Tuck offered a thin smile and took a step forward into the large lab, hoping to find Jamie himself. Paul moved forward, partially blocking his way. "Actually Jamie is out sick today."

Tuck frowned. He'd talked to Jamie the night before and he hadn't mentioned feeling ill. Poor kid—he was probably languishing at home right now.

Paul was watching him, a quizzical expression on his face.

As far as Tuck knew, no one at work was aware of their relationship and he'd just as soon keep it that way. He kept his voice noncommittal. "That's too bad. I hope he's better soon. No big deal, I'll email him. Thanks."

He himself had a vacation day and no desire to stop in at his own lab. He took the stairs, pulling out his cell phone as he went. So much for surprising Jamie at work. He'd surprise him in his sickbed instead and minister to him with hot chicken soup and a long, lingering blow job to distract him from whatever ailed him.

When he got to Jamie's place, he used his key and entered the small but bright living room. In case Jamie was sleeping, he didn't call out a greeting. Eager to see him, he stepped over the sill of the bedroom but instead of a sleeping Jamie, he saw the bed was neatly made, with no evidence of Jamie anywhere.

There was no one in the bathroom either. He walked through the small house, ending in the kitchen, which was empty and clean, not even a cup in the sink from morning coffee. Where was Jamie?

A sudden unwelcome thought slithered its way into his consciousness. Was Jamie with another man? Had he pretended to have work at his lab on Saturday in order to sneak off with some other guy the minute Tuck wasn't around?

Tuck shook his head. That was ridiculous and he knew it. Jamie had never given him the slightest reason to doubt his fidelity. They'd spent nearly all their spare time together, so when would he even have a chance to find someone new?

Shit, if anyone had been coveting someone else, it was him, mooning over Brendan and not even trying to hide it from Jamie. Jamie had been endlessly gracious and patient with him over that, and here he was, suspecting his lover the instant he couldn't track him down.

I'll just call him. What's the big deal? Maybe he decided to take a mental health day. Run some errands. Nothing wrong with that. He's not required to report his every move to me.

He flipped open his phone. It rang five times before going to voice mail. Tuck started to leave a message but decided he didn't want Jamie to feel he was checking up on him. They'd see each other soon enough.

"Just give me a few minutes alone with him, okay? Then he's all yours." Jamie put his hand on Brendan's thigh and squeezed. "You're doing the right thing, I promise. The right thing for all three of us. I'm proud of you."

Brendan smiled back uncertainly. "Let's just hope Tuck is on the same page."

"If he isn't, it'll be up to you to put him there."

Jamie climbed out of Brendan's car. They were parked in the parking lot of Tuck's apartment building, Jamie's motorcycle safely stowed in the U-Haul they'd rented for the purpose. They had left early that morning and driven straight through, stopping only to use the bathroom, stretch their legs and grab a sandwich for the road.

Jamie had called Tuck around seven thirty that evening to see when Tuck would be returning to Monterey. When Tuck told him he'd come home early and had wondered where Jamie was, Jamie had almost told him. Instead he said only, "I'll be home by nine. I'll tell you everything then."

"Are you okay, Jamie?" The warmth and concern in Tuck's voice nearly melted Jamie on the spot, but he'd only answered that he was fine and couldn't wait to see Tuck.

"Well, I'm at my place right now," Tuck informed him. "Want me to head over to Carmel?"

Jamie said no. He wanted Tuck to stay where he was. It would be better that way, given what Jamie had planned. *Please God, don't let me fuck this up. Don't let them fuck it up.*

Tuck had the door open before Jamie could get out his key. He took Jamie into his arms, not even bothering to close the door. They held each other close.

"I was worried, Jamie." Tuck spoke softly into Jamie's hair. "When you weren't at work and then I didn't hear from you..."

"I'm sorry, Tuck. I never meant to make you worry. I didn't realize you'd come home. I—I had somewhere I had to go."

"It's okay. As long as you're okay. As long as *we're* still okay." Tuck stepped back to look at him. Jamie saw the question in his dark, brooding eyes.

"Oh, Tuck. We're definitely okay. We're better than okay."

Tuck let out a deep breath. Jamie could feel his relief and felt bad for having made him worry.

Jamie turned to shut the door behind him.

"So are you going to tell me where you were?" Tuck's voice was light but Jamie sensed the tension still lingering.

"I went to see Brendan."

Tuck stared at him, a play of emotions washing over his face. Scowling, he demanded, "You what? Without me? Behind my back?"

"Without you, yeah. Behind your back, no. I realized I had to see him alone. It wasn't something I'd planned out beforehand, but when you left it just came to me it was what I had to do."

"Okay." Tuck said the word slowly, clearly still trying to work through just what was going on. He walked toward a chair and sank into it, crossing his arms protectively over his chest.

After hours in the car, Jamie didn't feel like sitting down. He paced in front of Tuck, determined to say what he had to say. "I love you, Tuck."

Tuck tilted his head at this apparent non sequitur. "What?"

"I said, I love you. I've never said it before. I wanted you to know that in no uncertain terms."

Tuck frowned. "Sure you have. We say it every day."

"No we don't. We say, 'love you' when we're saying goodbye. That's different."

"I guess you're right."

Jamie waited a beat, expecting, hoping Tuck would say it in return. Instead Tuck demanded, "Is this to do with Brendan? Did something happen I should know about? Don't fuck with me on this, Jamie. I swear to God."

Now it was Jamie's turn to frown. This wasn't going how he expected. He tried again. "I'm not trying to fuck with you. Yes, something happened you should know about. But not the way you mean. I didn't go there with the intention of seducing him behind your back, or anything like that."

Tuck gripped the arms of his chair and leaned forward, speaking earnestly. "I'm just confused, I guess, about why you felt you had to see Brendan without including me. I would have gone with you. Shit, I'm the one who wanted to contact him and you said to let it go."

"You're right. This wasn't a premeditated thing." Jamie paused, aware of the reproach in Tuck's words, trying to frame his thoughts. "Listen, what happened between us when we were stranded, it wasn't just about you and Brendan, or for that matter you and me. Maybe it started out that way, but it became about the three of us.

"That said, it was always you in the middle. You were the driving force, the attraction that held Brendan and me together. I mean, face it. If it had been just Brendan and me stuck there, no way would this have happened. I never could have penetrated his het reserve. I wouldn't have had the nerve to even try.

"And since we've been back, you've been the one pining for him. I don't mean that in a negative way. I mean, you're the one who couldn't let him go, who kept your love for him alive in your heart, while I was the supposedly sage one dispensing the wise advice to let him go."

Tuck started to respond but Jamie cut him off, eager to get it all out there. "I was lying to myself, Tuck. I was lying to you. I hadn't let him go either. I'd only tried to push him out of my heart because I was afraid of what it might mean for you and me. I was afraid if he came back onto the scene, the dynamic would shift again from us to you and him, with me relegated to the sidelines." He paused but forced himself to continue. "I guess I wanted you all to myself."

"So what made you change your mind? Why not just let his memory die a natural death?"

"You being gone. I had time to think. I realized I had to see him, face-to-face. At first I thought I was just going there to give him a piece of my mind. To demand who the fuck he thought he was to just disappear after what we'd shared. But when I got there, when I actually saw him, I realized I was fooling myself. I realized I was as in love with him as you are."

"You saw him..." Tuck's voice was wistful and filled with longing.

Jamie's heart constricted, a lingering fear of what he might be setting himself up for flaring again. He pushed it away, determined to move forward with his plan. If Tuck craved

Brendan over him, it was better to know now and cut his losses, however much it hurt.

He drew a deep breath and plunged on. "He's still in love with you, Tuck. He might be in love with me too. It's hard to know what he's really feeling and thinking at this point. But we definitely connected. I got some insight into him, into what makes him tick. He's been working through some pretty intense stuff about himself and who he is—you know, the kind of stuff most of us figure out in our teens or early twenties. Seems like he's just now getting to it."

"So what now? So you connected, that's great. You say he's in love with us, both of us. We love him, but he's a thousand miles away. Where do we go from here?"

Jamie closed his eyes, praying Tuck would be cool with what he was about to say. "He's here, Tuck. I brought him home with me. He's waiting to see you."

Color rose in Tuck's cheeks and he sat up straight, his hands clenched at his sides. "He's here? Now? Jamie, why didn't you tell me?"

"I wanted you to know first that I'd been there. That we'd connected on our own. That Brendan and I love each other, not because of you, or in spite of you, but as a part of what the three of us share. Or what we could share if we made the commitment."

Tuck was standing, pacing now as nervously as Jamie had been a moment before. "He's here? Where is he? Is he in the lobby? Don't tell me you made him wait on the back of your motorcycle."

"No, we drove down in his car, actually. We towed the motorcycle. He's down there probably going nuts by now. I didn't just want to spring him on you, unannounced."

Tuck looked so nervous it would have been comical if the

stakes weren't so high. Jamie moved toward him and took him into his arms. Tuck stood rather stiffly though at least he didn't pull away. Jamie kissed him lightly on the lips and dropped his arms, stepping back. "I did this for us, Tuck. Please say you understand."

He held his breath, part of him wishing he'd never gone to Seattle, though he knew in his heart he would do it again. Finally Tuck spoke. "Jamie. I love you too. Don't ever doubt it. And thank you. Thanks for doing what I should have done."

Jamie felt weak with relief. "I knew you'd understand." He opened his arms and this time Tuck stepped into them, wrapping him in a tight embrace. Jamie disengaged this time, worried now about how Brendan must be feeling alone in the car. "He's waiting. Let me go get him. It'll be better that way."

Tuck looked down at himself, stroked his stubbled cheek and ran his fingers through his hair. "Yeah, okay. Yeah." He was wearing a rumpled button-down shirt and a pair of denim shorts, his long, muscular legs bare.

Jamie laughed. "Don't worry, you look gorgeous. Touch of lipstick maybe, and you're good to go."

"Ha ha. Get out of here."

Jamie left the apartment, his heart tapping with nervous anticipation. Whatever happened next, it would be up to Tuck and Brendan.

Tuck changed from shorts to jeans, mainly for something to do. *It should have been me. I should have been the one to go to him.* And yet he hadn't. He could claim it was because Jamie had been so convincing that they should let it go, but he'd be lying to himself. Jamie hadn't even been in the picture the first time Tuck had let Brendan slip away.

After they'd connected that first time during the Blue

Glacier Project, he'd sent a few oblique half-hearted emails, hinting at his longing without ever coming out directly and telling Brendan the truth about his feelings.

When he'd had the great good luck of landing the polar research assignment, he'd blown it yet again, and would have lost Brendan for good if it hadn't been for the blizzard. It had taken Jamie, the youngest in years but perhaps the wisest or at least the most honest of the three, to confront Brendan and, hopefully, bring him back into their circle of love.

There was a soft knock at the door. He moved toward it, wondering why Jamie would bother to knock. His heart was beating too fast, his mind still trying to process the fact he was going to see Brendan in the flesh after two months of dreaming and missing him.

He opened the door and there Brendan stood, his blond, wavy hair flopping forward and curling over his ears, his gray green eyes wide. He was wearing a dark blue T-shirt beneath a khaki jacket, straight-legged black denim jeans hugging his legs and the sexy bulge at his crotch.

Tuck's heart skipped a beat and then began a strong, steady thrum. He took a deep breath. "Brendan. Hi."

"Hi." Brendan stood uncertainly. Tuck wanted to move forward and take him into his arms, but for some reason his feet were rooted to the ground.

Jamie would break the ice. Jamie would put them both at ease. Tuck peered around Brendan. "Where's Jamie?"

"He, uh, he sent me up here alone." Brendan looked sheepish and more anxious than ever. "Can I, uh, come in?"

Alone. What the hell? How could Jamie abandon him at a time like this? He needed Jamie's moral support. He needed his wry sense of humor to get them over the initial awkward stage.

Then it occurred to him what a show of trust it had been on

Jamie's part to leave the two of them alone, without trying to insert himself into their reunion in any way. He knew Tuck's strong feelings for Brendan. He knew the risk he was taking. Love welled up like a bright, hot fire, warming Tuck's heart. He stepped back, gesturing Brendan into the room.

Brendan entered and looked around the living room. Terracotta tile floors were scattered with brightly woven throw rugs. The sofa and two matching chairs were made from cherry wood and upholstered with overstuffed cushions of bright yellow. "This place is so you. Bright and colorful and full of light."

"Thanks." What was wrong with him? Brendan was here in the flesh at last. Why wasn't he grabbing him, kissing him, pushing him to the ground and tearing off his clothing? The man of his dreams had finally materialized like magic from the ether, and he couldn't seem to do anything but stare.

"I'm glad to see you, Tuck." Brendan spoke softly, not quite meeting Tuck's eye. Tuck opened his mouth to answer in kind but no words came. Brendan shifted, looking miserable. "Aren't you glad to see me?"

Suddenly Tuck realized what his problem was. He was pissed off. He was furious! He swallowed, trying to get a grip on his feelings. "To tell you the truth, I don't know what I am. I've been thinking about this moment, or something like it, for so long, I guess it just doesn't seem real. I mean, here you are. Hurrah. Jamie tells me you've seen the light. Admitted your sexual feelings for other men, accepted who you are at last, blah blah."

Brendan frowned, a line of consternation appearing between his eyes. "Blah, blah? Is that what this is to you, just a big bore? Do you have any idea the personal demons I've been grappling with over all this shit?"

"Of course I do. Maybe that's why I'm so pissed. It took you two months to get here, and you wouldn't be here now if it weren't for Jamie, am I right? You'd still be sitting alone in your house in Seattle, wrestling with your demons and feeling sorry for yourself, while the two guys who fell in love with you tried to get over you as best they could. While they tried to reconcile the man they'd come to know over those few amazing, wonderful days with the closed-off, repressed jerk on the phone who claimed none of it mattered, none of it was real. Just a passing perversion shared by desperate men in desperate times. We were just supposed to accept that and go on with our lives, forgetting you ever existed."

Brendan sat down heavily in a chair and stared at the floor. Tuck sat opposite him, aware he was being horrible, wishing he could undo it and start over. Brendan looked up slowly. His face was pale, his expression stricken.

"You're right. About everything you said. I tried to deny it, both the import of what we'd shared, and my own feelings about it. I was a coward and a jackass. And it didn't just affect you. Because of my inability to face some truths, my ex-girlfriend got dragged back into things and I hurt her all over again.

"I guess what they say is true—sometimes you have to smack up against a brick wall before you can admit it's time to change or die. For me the death was an emotional one. It's taken me this long to figure out I was killing myself by shutting off my true feelings and desires.

"I've come to realize I've spent a lifetime ignoring whole chunks of myself. If feelings didn't fit in with my carefully constructed view of the world and my place in it, I just shut them down. I don't have anyone or anything to blame, unless you can blame a whole society and the way men are taught to look at and approach the world."

Tuck thought one could indeed blame society for precisely that defect, but he said nothing, aware Brendan needed to talk without interruption. While he had had Jamie to work things through with over the last two months, he could only imagine how alone the self-contained Brendan must have felt.

Brendan continued. "When we connected last summer, I *knew* there was something there. I knew it was more than just a spontaneous friendship between colleagues. Even then, though I could barely admit it to myself, much less anyone else, I had fallen for you. Then I got scared of my feelings and shut them down. Even so, when I saw you on the roster of research candidates for the polar project, my heart leapt.

"But then during the project I reverted to my usual mindless, soulless M.O. I shut down and focused on work, telling myself the situation wasn't conducive to exploring any unresolved feelings I might have toward you. So I let it go. You and Jamie somehow broke through the barriers when we were stranded, but as soon as we were rescued, the old walls rose again, hemming me in.

"I'm not sure if I would have found the courage to reach out to you and Jamie again, but then Jamie just appeared, like in a fairytale where if you wish hard enough, your dreams come true. I was at a point where I was finally ready to admit some hard truths and then, there he was, holding out his hand to me, offering me another chance."

Brendan stood and stepped forward, reaching out his hand to Tuck. "I have no right to ask, but will you give me that chance as well? Let me try again? This time I won't walk away, Tuck, unless you want me to. I understand now what I gave up. It wasn't just your love, but a chance to finally be myself."

Tuck's heart seemed to expand, pressing against the confines of his chest. He took Brendan's offered hand, allowing the other man to pull him up. They moved into each other's arms and held one another tight. Tuck inhaled the other man's scent, reveling in his closeness, awe falling over him and washing away any remaining anger.

They kissed, tentatively at first, then with more conviction, finally with a kind of desperation. Tuck pushed at Brendan's jacket and Brendan shrugged out of it, letting it fall.

They sank together to the sofa, pulling at each other's clothing, their mouths hungrily seeking each other. "Tuck." Brendan managed to infuse the word with such meaning—anguish, regret, longing, desire. He tugged hard at Tuck's shirt, jerking it open in a spray of buttons. "Oh. I'm sorry. I didn't mean to—"

Tuck put his fingers to Brendan's lips. "It doesn't matter." He reached for the hem of Brendan's shirt, dragging it up over his head. They sat bare-chested, face-to-face, drinking each other in.

Brendan shook his tousled hair from his eyes. "I'm sorry, Tuck. For everything."

"I know," Tuck whispered. "But you're here now. Kiss me again." It felt so right to hold Brendan, to taste him, to feel the press of his bone-hard erection. If only Jamie were there to share it with them. Jamie. Where was Jamie now? Tuck eased away from Brendan's kiss and stood, suddenly longing for Jamie with an almost physical ache.

"Where's Jamie? He's not still down in the car, is he?"

"No. He went home. Back to his place in Carmel. Said he was going to shower and rest."

"Did he say we should come over?"

"He didn't say. I think he was leaving it to us."

They looked at each other. No discussion was needed. Tuck

read Brendan's feelings on his face and was sure his were just as transparent. Of one accord, they stood. Brendan reached for his shirt.

"I'll be right back." Tuck hurried to his bedroom to grab a fresh shirt. He returned to the living room, pulling it over his head. "I picked a T-shirt this time, just in case you can't control yourself again."

Brendan grinned. "Sorry. It's your fault for being so fucking hot."

They stood smiling at one another a moment and then recalled their mission. "Jamie," they said in unison. Without another word, they hurried out the door.

Chapter Eighteen

Brendan followed Tuck along a stone path that led from the narrow driveway to the small cottage nearly hidden behind tall shade trees. Though it was dark, he could hear the crash of waves along the shore that couldn't be very far away.

"This is some place." They stepped onto the lit porch, which held two white rocking chairs. Brendan imagined the two of them, Tuck and Jamie, sitting there watching the sun set over the water. A sense of longing tugged at his heart.

"Yeah. Jamie inherited it from his uncle. We mostly stay here." Tuck knocked lightly on the screen door while Brendan took in the import of his statement. These two were a couple. Was there really room for three?

Jamie pulled open the door, a wide grin on his face. His hair was wet, his blue eyes made even bluer by the turquoise silk shirt he wore, the first several buttons undone to reveal his smooth, tan chest.

"Hey. I was wondering if you guys were going to show up. I made some frozen margaritas and I was just sitting here thinking I might have to drink the whole pitcher by myself." He held up a glass half filled with pale green slush and flashed a dimpled grin.

They entered the room. Brendan stood back while Tuck and Jamie embraced. He looked around the small living room, with its wide-planked blond hardwood floors and wicker furniture. There was a small fireplace with a thick rug in front of it. Though it was only early May, Brendan imagined a fire crackling in the hearth, the three of them naked on the soft rug in front of it.

Jamie and Tuck parted and Jamie turned to Brendan. "Hey, stranger. Welcome to California."

"This place is great. You must be right on the ocean."

"Yep. A few hundred yards down the hill and there you are. I was incredibly lucky to get this. All sorts of relatives were furious when they were passed over in favor of the little faggot nephew." His eyes narrowed briefly and Brendan thought how everyone had a story and he'd love to get to know both Jamie's and Tuck's better.

Jamie's scowl was quickly replaced by a laugh. "What can I say? Uncle Rob and I were like this." He held up a hand, the first two fingers crossed.

They followed Jamie into the kitchen, where he filled two large wineglasses with the frozen margarita mix and topped off his own. "Let's sit on the porch," Jamie suggested.

When they stepped out into the cool night air, Brendan noticed the stack of wooden folding chairs leaning up against the wall on the far side of the porch. Jamie placed one beside the rockers and sat, with Brendan beside him and Tuck on Brendan's other side.

Brendan rocked in his chair, sipping the frozen, tart lime drink, still not quite taking in where he was and who he was with. If Jamie hadn't miraculously appeared on his doorstep the morning before, he'd be in his bed now, reading one of Walter Mosley's Easy Rawlins murder mysteries and trying desperately to keep his inherent loneliness at bay.

He glanced at Jamie. He was staring past the trees to the

glimmer of ocean beyond, sparkling silver beneath a full moon. Brendan wondered what he was thinking.

He'd greeted them so easily when they'd come to his door. Clearly by his attire and the pitcher of drinks, he was expecting them to return, but he had no guarantee. He'd driven all that way to tell Brendan both he and Tuck were in love with him, then he'd brought him home to Tuck and left them alone.

What an act of courage on his part. Jamie knew better than anyone but himself and Tuck of their intense and, until now, unresolved feelings for each other. They hadn't fallen into bed without him, but they might have.

Brendan marveled silently. He'd completely underestimated Jamie, assuming he was just another young, sexy guy out to have fun with whoever was available. Now he honestly couldn't say who he loved more—Tuck or Jamie. A thought began to form, one he was almost afraid to explore. Maybe he didn't have to choose?

He looked over at Tuck, at his strong profile and his easy, relaxed posture. Had Tuck really forgiven him? He'd wasted nearly a year of their lives by denying his own feelings for so long. Well, there was nothing to be done about what was past. All he could do was focus on the present, and be as honest as he could going forward, not just with the two of them, but with himself.

"I love the sound of the ocean." Tuck's deep voice pulled Brendan from his thoughts. Tuck added, "It always puts me to sleep." To emphasize his words, he yawned.

Was that a hint? Just in case, Brendan offered, "I should get a motel room or something. Let you guys get some rest. You both have to work in the morning, right?"

"You'll do no such thing," Tuck retorted. "We finally got you back. We aren't letting you go again, right, Jamie?"

Jamie nodded. "You got that right. We'll tie you to the bed if we have to."

"Yeah." Tuck laughed and winked. "Jamie's into bondage. We just bought some cool leather wrist and ankle cuffs. We'll cuff you to the bed while we're gone so you can't escape."

Brendan raised his eyebrows, half embarrassed, half turned-on. Despite himself, his cock rose at the image of Jamie, naked and cuffed to a bed. He looked at Jamie, intrigued by the sudden flush in his cheeks. Confident, cocky Jamie with the tattoo and the Harley was the last guy he would have pegged as being into that sort of thing, at least not on the receiving end.

Tuck laughed. "I think we've got Brendan's attention." He was staring pointedly at Brendan's crotch. Now it was Brendan's turn to blush. To deflect attention, he pursued his earlier comment. "Seriously, though. It's nearly eleven. Don't you both have to be at your labs in the morning?"

"Not till nine," Tuck answered. "What about you? What arrangements did you make with your lab and your students back in Seattle?"

"Family emergency. I took the week off. I have a ton of vacation time saved. It wasn't a problem."

Jamie reached over the arm of Brendan's rocking chair, leaving a trail of electricity along Brendan's thigh as he moved toward his crotch. Tuck's hand dropped to his other thigh. Brendan's cock strained beneath the denim, his balls tightening.

"Let's go inside," Tuck said softly.

Jamie led the way, with Brendan in the middle and Tuck following behind. Jamie took their glasses and headed into the kitchen. Brendan started to move toward the chairs in the living room but Tuck stopped him.

"Let's go into the bedroom."

"I thought maybe we could talk—"

"We've talked enough."

Jamie came back and, as if it were prearranged, they flanked him on either side and led Brendan into the bedroom. It was larger than he'd expected, nearly the size of the living room, with a king-sized bed set in a four-poster black wrought iron frame.

He realized both Tuck and Jamie were removing their clothes, Jamie unbuttoning his silk shirt, Tuck shucking his T-shirt and jeans. In a moment they were both naked and turning their attentions to him.

Tuck took the hem of Brendan's shirt, lifting it over his head while Jamie knelt at his feet, removing first his shoes and socks and then reaching for his fly. Shyness assailed Brendan when Jamie tugged at his boxers, but he didn't resist him. After all, the other two were already naked, their cocks rising along with his.

Tuck pulled Brendan toward him and kissed him, slow and tender. "Don't leave us again, 'kay, Bren? Please."

Jamie was behind him, cocooning him between the two of them. "Yeah," Jamie added. "Stay and let us love you."

Warmth and happiness suffused him. He could have stood there all night, locked safely in their arms.

Jamie stepped back and Tuck guided Brendan to the bed. Gently he pressed him down to the mattress. They lay on either side. When Tuck leaned over him, Brendan noticed for the first time the small jagged scar, white against smooth olive skin. He reached up to trace its outline with his finger, recalling that horrible, wonderful time they'd spent together, awed to be back with the two people he realized mattered most in his life.

Tuck smiled but said nothing. Instead he lowered his face to kiss Brendan's lips. Jamie scooted lower, leaving a trail of butterfly kisses over Brendan's chest and stomach. Brendan's cock was aching, the blood thrumming in his veins.

Tuck spoke. "I want to make love to you, Brendan. I've been dreaming of this moment for a long time. Having Jamie here only makes it better. Do you want it too? Are you ready to take that final step with us?"

Brendan swallowed hard, his pulse quickening. "Yes," he managed. "I want it." To think, only a few nights before, he'd sat alone, drunk on the couch, using a dildo on himself and fantasizing about just such a moment as this. Was this really happening? Or would he wake up, his cock hard, his arms empty, as he had so many times before?

But it was no dream. Tuck rose to a sitting position and reached toward a small black lacquered box on the nightstand. He pulled out a condom and tore its wrapper, expertly rolling it over his erect shaft.

He pushed Brendan's shoulder, indicating he should roll over. "I think it will be easiest for you on your hands and knees. So Jamie can be underneath you to, uh, distract you, if necessary."

Not quite sure what he meant, but deeply aroused by the realization of what was about to happen, Brendan scrambled to his hands and knees. Tuck, still sitting on the bed beside him, took a tube of lubricant from the nightstand and squirted some onto his fingers. He positioned himself behind Brendan, who took a deep breath.

"Relax." Tuck's voice was soothing. Brendan startled a little when a lubricated finger ran a light ring around the rim of his hole. Despite Tuck's gentle admonition, he stiffened when the finger entered his nether passage, gently pushing its way inside him.

Meanwhile Jamie maneuvered himself until his head was

directly below Brendan's cock, his body perpendicular beneath Brendan. Jamie lifted his head from the bed, closing his mouth over the crown of Brendan's throbbing cock. He held it with his lips while stroking the length of it with his tongue.

A second finger was added but Brendan found he didn't mind at all. Jamie was indeed distracting him and it felt fantastic. After several minutes of the sensual frigging, Tuck leaned over him, his mouth close to Brendan's ear.

"I'll go as slow as you need. We have all the time in the world. You ready for me, babe?"

Jamie chose that moment to catch his balls in a delicious grip, his mouth still glued to Brendan's cock.

"Yes," he breathed. "I'm ready. I want you."

"I want you too. So much." Tuck touched the head of his cock to the nether entrance and pressed. There was a split second of pain and then merely a fullness. Tuck moved carefully, inching his way into Brendan's passage.

Brendan kept waiting for the pain to recur, but it didn't. Jamie's mouth and hands were driving him to distraction. The realization that Tuck was fucking him made his cock all the harder. Tuck began to move in tantalizing circles, still only the head of his shaft inside.

"You good?" Tuck murmured, his voice thick with lust.

"Yeah. Yeah, it's good." Brendan dared to push back against the huge phallus inside him. Still no pain, only a sensual fullness. Taking courage, he pushed back harder and this time Tuck moved forward to meet him, burying himself deep inside.

Each sensual thrust by Tuck was met with Jamie's fingers and lips stroking Brendan's cock beneath him. Brendan tried to hold himself back. He wanted to savor the moment, to draw it out, to never come down from the incredible high he was experiencing. But it was only a matter of minutes before the combined attentions of the two sexy men drove him over the edge.

"Oh God," he cried out, desperately trying to hold on just a little longer. Tuck was thrusting hard against him, Jamie's tongue and hands rendering him nearly senseless. He jerked hard. Strong hands pulled him back, impaling him on Tuck's sword of a cock while he spurted in a series of ecstatic thrusts into Jamie's willing mouth. He could feel Tuck coming at the same time, jerking in tandem to his own shuddering spasms. It was the most incredible feeling to know another man was coming deep inside him.

Completely spent, his muscles gave way all at once and he found himself tumbling forward against the bed. Jamie swiveled adroitly from beneath him while Tuck collapsed on top of him.

They lay in a tangle of sweaty limbs for what seemed a long while, Brendan passing in and out of a sexual lethargy that had rendered him paralyzed. Tuck finally lifted himself from him and rolled away.

Brendan, whose eyes were already closed, felt himself being pulled down into an inexorable sleep. He fought it, forcing his eyes to open and attempting to lift himself up. He failed, his eyes again closing, the lids weighted down with exhaustion and satiation. Dimly he was aware of the murmur of masculine voices above him but he couldn't make out the words.

He would rest, just for a while...

When Brendan next opened his eyes, he was confused. Sunlight filled the room and the bed was empty. Had he really slept the night through? He sat up abruptly and heard the sound of running water.

Just then Tuck entered the bedroom from what must be

the bathroom, wearing bikini underwear and nothing else. His black hair was wet and combed back. "Good morning. It's still early. We don't have to get up for work yet." He slipped into the covers beside Brendan.

"I can't believe I slept through the night. I must have been more tired than I thought."

"You didn't move the whole night." Tuck grinned good-naturedly. "We considered mouth-to-mouth resuscitation but we decided to have pity on you."

Jamie emerged from the bathroom with only a small towel around his waist. "Hey there, Bren. Did you sleep well?"

"Like a log, though I can't believe it. I usually can't sleep in any bed but my own."

Jamie moved toward them and dropped his towel, slipping naked into the bed on Brendan's other side.

Brendan saw something out of the corner of his eye attached to the bedpost over Jamie's head. It was a black leather cuff, secured by a Velcro strap to the wrought iron. He looked toward the other post, where a second cuff dangled. "Oh my God," he blurted. "You weren't kidding about the cuffs."

"Did you think we were?" Tuck's voice held a seductive, dangerous edge Brendan had never heard before, but which made his cock stiffen with interest. Tuck drew a finger over Brendan's cheek and moved it slowly down his throat. "Jamie finds it very...stimulating. And it turns me on too—knowing he can't get away, no matter what I do."

"Ooh." The word was pulled from Brendan, awe and arousal whipping through his blood at the thought of these two hot men playing their bondage games. Jamie reached beneath the sheets, finding and grabbing Brendan's telltale erection.

"Would you like to try it, Brendan? To see what it's like to be helpless and at the mercy of two strong men?"

214

"No. No, not me. No, sir." Brendan's heart had begun to pound.

Jamie's fingers curled tighter around Brendan's shaft. "His lips say no, no, no, but his cock says yes, yes, yes."

"Come on." Tuck's seductive tone sent shivers down Brendan's spine. "Try it. Just for fun. Something tells me you'll like it. If you don't, we'll let you go. Won't we, Jamie?"

Jamie stroked Brendan's cock, using the pre-come at its tip to lubricate his fingers. "Yeah. Absolutely."

They each took an arm, lifting Brendan's wrists into the cuffs and securing them snugly in the leather. Brendan's mouth was suddenly dry. He could have told them to stop, but he didn't. He tugged at the restraints, his heart beating a mile a minute.

"He looks kind of nervous." Jamie's voice was teasing.

"Yeah. He does at that. Think we should let him go?"

"I don't know. Maybe we better ask him. This could just be a decoy." Jamie pulled back the sheets to reveal Brendan's raging erection. His grip sent shivers of pleasure through Brendan's body, even while he blushed.

"You're right. We don't want to hold him against his will." Tuck leaned over, licking a circle around one of Brendan's nipples and then lightly biting the nubbin at its center. At the same moment, Jamie lowered his mouth over the head of Brendan's cock.

"Ah, Lord." Brendan moaned. He pulled again at the cuffs, aware he was well and truly restrained. His cock elongated in Jamie's wet embrace.

Tuck lifted his head. "So what about it, Bren? Should we let you out of those cuffs? Hmm?" He licked and bit the second nipple while Jamie took the length of Brendan's cock deeper, nearly making him come then and there.

"I...I..." He struggled to catch his breath and realized he was gasping. He tried again. "If...if...oh. Oh. Yeah..." He forgot the question and the answer as Tuck's lips closed over his, his tongue slipping into his mouth.

Jamie was working dark, delicious magic on his cock, driving him nearly out of his mind with pleasure while Tuck engaged him in a leisurely, sensuous kiss. Automatically he reached to wrap his arms around Tuck and pull him closer, but the cuffs prevented him from doing so. All he could do was lie there, submitting to Tuck's melting kiss and Jamie's fiery tongue rippling over his cock.

He tried to twist his head from beneath Tuck's, to warn them he was about to come. He didn't want to come, not yet, not like some teenager, but he couldn't help it. Tuck held his head, kissing him deep and hard while Jamie's focus was relentless.

Insistent fingers caressed his tightening balls while lips and tongue converged on his throbbing shaft. He tugged at the cuffs, a prisoner to the onslaught of exhilarating sensation hurtling through every fiber of his body.

He gurgled against Tuck's mouth and gave in to the furious beat of ecstatic blood pulsing through his veins. His body convulsed, arching up against Jamie's mouth and hands as he tumbled into orgasm.

Chapter Nineteen

Jamie and Tuck both pulled away at the same time. Jamie's eyes were watering. He wiped at them while still swallowing the remnants of Brendan's seed. He looked at Tuck, whose dark eyes were shining, the tip of his tongue showing between parted lips.

They turned toward Brendan who lay limp, eyes closed, mouth open. He looked incredibly hot, his thickly muscled arms pulled taut, his broad chest tapering to a narrow waist and the thick cock, now at half-mast against dark blond curls. He opened his eyes and looked from Tuck to Jamie.

Jamie well understood the burning, fierce light he saw there. He knew the orgasm they'd given him had been rendered tenfold more exciting by the restraints. He recognized in Brendan's ardent reaction that Brendan, like himself, was deeply aroused by the sensual helplessness engendered by the cuffs.

In their time together so far, Tuck and he had experimented with bondage from both sides. Tuck had permitted Jamie to bind him by wrist and ankle to the bedposts, but there had been no thrill. Tuck didn't seem to have whatever gene it was that turned vanilla sex into molten passion when one was bound and at the erotic mercy of another. Brendan, on the other hand, was obviously a kindred spirit in that regard.

Tuck seemed to read Jamie's thoughts by giving voice to this observation. "He's as into that as you are, huh, Jamie? Maybe more so." He rubbed his hands together with glee. "Just think of the fun I can have with the two of you. The erotic possibilities stagger the mind."

"Hey," Brendan said weakly. He cleared his throat. "Let me out of these cuffs, will you?"

"I don't know." Tuck grinned evilly. "I kind of like having you there, naked and bound. Maybe we'll tie down your ankles too. Leave you that way a while as punishment for making us wait so long to have you back again."

"Very funny. Let me go." Brendan jerked against the cuffs but Jamie noted with amusement that his cock, despite the recent orgasm, was twitching with interest.

Tuck leaned up and released the cuffs. Brendan's arms fell heavily to the bed. Tuck sidled beside him and Jamie lay on his other side. They each took an arm, massaging the life back into it in short order.

The sound of a clock chiming in the living room made Tuck sit up. "Shit. It's eight o'clock already. We have to go, Jamie."

Jamie swung his legs over the side of the bed. If he hadn't called in sick the day before he wouldn't go in, but he didn't dare do it twice in a row. "There are bathing suits in that drawer." He pointed toward the dresser. "Beach towels are on the bottom shelf of the linen closet in the bathroom. Feel free to go down to the beach while we're gone. There's plenty of food in the fridge and we'll be home before you know it."

"I wish we didn't have to go." Tuck stroked Brendan's cheek.

"It's okay," Brendan replied. "I probably need the time to recuperate from you two. You're going to kill me at this pace."

218

"But it's a damn good way to die, huh?" Jamie quipped.

Jamie had expected the day to drag, as eager as he was to return home to Brendan and Tuck. However he soon found himself caught up in his work, fascinated with the results of a complex experiment that was finally coming to fruition. When Tuck texted him on his cell phone that he'd meet him in five minutes at the car garage, Jamie was stunned to realize how much time had passed.

When they got home, they found Brendan sitting on the porch, wearing a pair of Jamie's swim trunks, evidence of the sun on his bare shoulders and chest. He looked, Jamie thought, good enough to eat.

Brendan had prepared a meal for them, hamburgers and french fries, along with a green salad. He served it proudly, along with a bottle of red wine. Jamie fondly recalled Brendan's one specialty at the polar lab, spaghetti and meatballs. So the man had two meals under his belt, he thought with an inward grin.

After dinner, they took a long walk along the shore, talking about their research and the latest news. Jamie marveled at how right it felt, the three of them together, talking about their day as if they'd been together for years.

They returned to the house and shared a second glass of red wine before retiring to the bedroom, each aware it had all been leading back to this.

In short order the three of them again lay naked in the big, comfortable bed, this time with Tuck in the middle. Tuck turned toward Jamie and they gazed into one another's eyes. The love Jamie saw there took his breath away. At that moment, the last vestige of jealousy over the connection between Tuck and Brendan slipped away for good.

Jamie had known he was taking a gamble when he had

sent Brendan up alone to see Tuck the night before. After all, the two shared a history, however unrealized, that had predated him. He'd returned to his cottage to shower and shave. He'd dressed and made the drinks, but had been prepared, or so he told himself, to spend a quiet evening alone on his porch, letting the sea lull him into a peaceful reverie.

If they had chosen to remain at Tuck's place, too caught up in finding each other again, he wanted to believe he could have handled it. Happily, he hadn't been faced with that eventuality. They had come home to him.

Jamie was, for the first time in his life, truly in love. He knew, too, that Tuck loved him with all his heart. So where did Brendan fit in? He looked over at the sexy, blond man and his heart surged with affection. Was it love? If it wasn't, he knew in his bones the seeds for a love as deep and abiding as he already felt for Tuck were there.

If only Brendan could find the courage to remain in the moment with them. If he didn't run and hide again, the three of them might find something truly unique together. He glanced at Tuck, who was regarding him with those dark, perfect eyes. It was as if Tuck had a direct conduit to his mind and heart.

"I want you." The words thrilled Jamie, as they always did when Tuck uttered them. Wordlessly he reached for a condom and lovingly slid it over Tuck's already-erect cock. Brendan moved apart from them, his eyes hooded as he watched Jamie roll to his hands and knees while Tuck positioned himself behind him.

Tuck used his fingers, opening and relaxing Jamie's ass for his large cock. Jamie, aching for the onslaught, groaned and pushed back against the slick, lubricated fingers pressing their way into him. He was aware of Brendan's burning eyes.

Tuck's hard cock took the place of his fingers, carefully but relentlessly entering him, spreading him, claiming him. Strong hands on his hips held him in place as Tuck filled him. A rich, buttery warmth spread through his body as Tuck began to move. He loved having Tuck inside him.

He felt the warm grip of Tuck's hand, stroking his cock, and he moaned with pleasure. Tuck pulled him back hard, both hands on his hips. He realized then the hand on his cock must belong to Brendan.

"Get on your knees too, Bren." Tuck's voice was hoarse with lust. "I want you to be a part of this. I want to claim you through Jamie."

Jamie understood in a flash what Tuck was saying and his cock, already hard, stiffened to the nth degree. Brendan didn't move at once, perhaps slower to grasp what Tuck intended, or else just resistant.

"Grab a condom. Put it on Jamie." Tuck's voice had slipped into the erotic tone of command he assumed when employing his brand of gentle but deeply arousing sexual dominance. Jamie's cock pulsed in anticipation. He held his breath, waiting to see if Brendan would obey.

To his delight, Brendan reached for a condom. He tore open the packet and rolled it over Jamie's shaft, his fingers trembling. "Good," Tuck crooned. "Now on your knees. Offer that sexy ass to Jamie and to me."

Bren didn't move for a long, frozen moment, during which he stared at Tuck, his eyes blazing, his chest heaving. Tuck stared back, his powerful, erotic will like a palpable force in the room.

Brendan dropped his gaze and crawled on his hands and knees to position himself in front of Jamie. Jamie draped himself over Brendan's back, just holding him for a while as Tuck, still buried inside him, began to move again.

"Here." Tuck pressed the tube of lubricant against Jamie's arm. Jamie moved back and took it, squeezing some onto his fingertips. He smeared it over his cock and leaned again over Brendan.

"You good, Brendan? This is okay with you?"

Brendan twisted his head back, his eyes glittering. "Yeah."

Tuck remained still, deep inside Jamie but not moving while Jamie stroked and teased Brendan's puckered hole with his fingers. The muscles eased with his gentle attentions. He withdrew his fingers and moved forward, nestling the crown of his shaft between Brendan's spread ass cheeks.

He felt Brendan tense and leaned up over him, his voice soft and coaxing. "It's okay, Bren. You're doing great. This is so fucking hot. I've always wanted to be in the middle like this. Do it for me."

"For us," Tuck said behind him, swiveling inside him in a way that made Jamie moan and push back wantonly against him.

Brendan moved back ever so slightly, a silent cue for Jamie to continue. Carefully he pressed against the tight passageway, grunting with pleasure as the muscle gave way and allowed him entrance.

Brendan stiffened. Jamie kissed him on the shoulder. "Just relax." He reached around Brendan's body to find and capture his cock in his hand. A few strokes were sufficient to return it to full erection. Brendan sighed his pleasure. Jamie pushed forward carefully, his cock caught in the hot, tight glove of Brendan's passage.

When he was fully inside Brendan, he turned back to Tuck and nodded. Tuck began to move again, pulling nearly out of him before thrusting back, driving Jamie's body against Brendan's, forcing his cock deeper into him.

Jamie gripped Brendan's cock, pumping it as Tuck thrust in and out of him. They began to move in tandem. Tuck held him tight, his fingers gripping Jamie's hips as he pummeled him, pushing and pulling Jamie's body onto his cock. Each thrust forced Jamie's cock deep into Brendan.

The room was ripe with the scent of sex and the sounds of grunting, panting men. Jamie was lost in sensation, awash in lust, no longer conscious of himself as a separate being. He was part of Tuck, an extension of his lover, guided and controlled by Tuck's movements, a direct conduit from Tuck to Brendan.

They were three lovers brought together by their passion, as close at that moment as it was possible to be. Jamie was freefalling, surrendering to the sensations overtaking him from all sides. Tuck began to ejaculate inside him, his breathy cries punctuating each thrust. This set off a chain reaction. Jamie knew he was nearing the edge of no return.

Somehow he managed to keep his hand on Brendan's cock. As he moved inside Brendan, he felt the sticky evidence of Brendan's release against his fingers. Then conscious thought was obliterated by the most blindingly intense orgasm of his life, ripping through his body like liquid fire.

When he came to himself a few seconds later, he was still held aloft by the two men, one in front, one behind, their bodies slick with sweat, their hearts beating on either side of him in time to his own.

It was Saturday morning, the sky a perfect cerulean blue, the air fresh and clear. Tuck and Jamie stood watching as Brendan drove away, waving his farewell. They'd spent an incredible five days together, both Jamie and Tuck getting out of their labs as soon as they could each afternoon to race home to Brendan.

Brendan spent his time alone lazing on the beach, straightening the house and cooking them dinner. After sharing the meal and good conversation, they invariably removed to the bedroom, hungry for more than food.

The sex had been amazing, each new exploration more exciting than the last. Brendan was as hot for the cuffs and ties as Jamie was. They'd improvised, using the ankle cuffs on Brendan's wrists so Tuck could tether both of them at once to the head of the bed and fuck them, alternating between the two until he exhausted himself with pleasure. Tuck teasingly began to refer to the pair as his two willing slave boys, though the play was light and the bondage mild.

But it wasn't only the bright, hot sweetness of their ménage that bound them together. Brendan was fast becoming an integral part of their lives, or so it felt to Tuck. Yet from the moment Brendan had arrived, Tuck knew the time would come when Brendan would have to leave. He had his life and his work back in Seattle, and a long drive ahead of him.

He'd said he'd be back. Brendan had already put out feelers at Wexler for a position, and at the university as well. With Brendan's credentials and reputation, Tuck doubted he would have a problem relocating. If that's what he really wanted to do.

Despite himself, Tuck couldn't forget how ardent and passionate Brendan had been while they'd been stranded, and then how cold and shut down he'd become so soon after. Though it was hard to imagine the same scenario playing itself out again, Tuck well knew the power of denial.

Once alone again, returned to his own familiar territory and patterns of behavior, would Brendan convince himself yet again that what they'd shared was only the stuff of fantasy? Would he try to force himself back into his straight persona, determined to put the memories of Tuck and Jamie behind him once and for all?

Once Brendan's car was out of sight, Jamie and Tuck dropped arms and walked up to the porch. They sat side by side on the rockers, staring past the trees to the shore beyond.

"Let's go down and have a swim later, want to?" Jamie suggested.

"Yeah, that sounds good."

"Don't worry, Tuck."

"About what?" He glanced away, unsettled by Jamie's uncanny ability to read his mind.

"He'll be back."

"How do you know?"

"Some things you just know. He'll be back. Maybe not next week, but soon and for good. He's a part of us. It's no longer just about him, or about us. We're a threesome now. More than a couple plus one. More than a ménage. We belong together. It's all good."

"I agree with you. But how do you know he does?"

"I saw it in his eyes."

All at once Tuck saw Brendan's beautiful gray green eyes in his mind. There had been tears in them when they'd embraced, but beyond the tears, something else. Jamie was right. There had been promise in them.

Still, Tuck couldn't resist saying, "And what if he doesn't?"

"If he doesn't..." Jamie's cheeks dimpled, "...then we'll just hop on my Harley and go get him. Don't forget, I know where he lives."

Tuck laughed and nodded. "Meanwhile, we can buy a third rocking chair for the porch." He dropped his hand lightly to

225

Jamie's thigh. After a moment Jamie's hand covered his. Tuck's heart was full to bursting. Jamie was right. It was all good.

"Dr. Aaronson."

"Brendan. Glad I caught you. It's Horace. Horace Greeley."

"Horace. It's great to hear from you." Horace Greeley was the chief scientist and head of Wexler Institute where Jamie and Tuck worked.

The week before, while still in California with the guys, Brendan had made a visit to the facility, letting it be known he was considering a move and was interested in possibilities. Horace had been out of town at the time.

Brendan had met Horace at a symposium where he'd given a paper on his research two years before. Horace had sought him out, going so far as to offer him a position with his own lab and full staff if he'd consider relocating. At the time he'd shrugged it off, happy where he was.

Brendan realized he was clutching the receiver. He eased his grip and waited to hear what Horace had to say. "I heard you were possibly interested in moving down to this neck of the woods. If that's still the case, the timing couldn't be better. We just got funding for an exciting new project that will study the diffusion-controlled metabolism for long-term survival of single isolated microorganisms trapped within polar ice cores. We have a topnotch young guy, David Tucker, who is also regarded as something of an expert in the field of deep ice cores. I was thinking of pulling him for the project. Do you know him?"

"Yeah. I know him. Great guy. We worked together most recently on the Antarctic Deep Ice project." Brendan strove to keep his voice neutral, trying to contain the bubbling joy rising in his heart just at the mention of Tuck's name.

"Yes, yes, of course. So then, are you interested? We're ready to take you onboard as soon as you're available."

Brendan was grinning so hard his cheeks hurt. "Horace, I'd be delighted. Count me in."

They spoke a while longer and made arrangements for a face-to-face meeting to iron out the details. Horace made noises about adequate compensation. Brendan didn't tell him he'd pay for the chance to work at Wexler—anything to make it possible to be with Jamie and Tuck.

Brendan hung up the phone and swiveled in his chair to face the window. It was happening. His dreams were clicking into place. He savored the knowledge for several minutes while he calmed himself down enough to make the call.

Turning back to his desk, he reached for the phone. Tuck answered on the second ring. "Hello?"

"Tuck, it's Brendan. I'm coming home."

About the Author

Claire Thompson lives and writes in upstate New York. She has written over forty novels, many dealing with the romance of erotic submission, along with a newfound passion for m/m erotica.

To learn more about Claire Thompson, please visit www.clairethompson.net. Send an email to Claire at Claire@clairethompson.net and sign up for her newsletter to keep abreast of her latest work, events, happenings and contests.

Sure, the sex is scorching hot, but can three hearts truly beat as one?

Our Man Friday
© 2008 Claire Thompson

What's the old adage—sex ruins friendship? Cassidy lives it every day as she fights the lingering feelings for her ex, Ian. Still secretly, desperately in love with him, she settles for sharing a house and a business. Their lives are intertwined in every way...except the way she wants most.

Fear of commitment drove Ian to push his and Cassidy's romance back into his comfort zone—friendship. But things become decidedly uncomfortable when sexy Scotsman Kye McClellan enters the picture. As Cassidy's passion reignites, Ian is faced with the sudden prospect of losing the thing most precious to him.

Ian remains firmly in Cassidy's heart even as she succumbs to Kye's charms. Soon, as Kye's allure draws Ian in, she begins to wonder if she can have all she's ever wanted—plus one. Just as they all begin to tip into the white-hot cauldron of romance, Kye takes to his wanderlusting ways to avoid the burn. Ian and Cassidy are left with each other...and an even bigger missing piece than before.

All they can do is trust that love will somehow bring their gypsy-hearted lover home again.

Warning: Explicit, erotic m/m/f passion. Double penetration takes on a whole new meaning—the hot and sensual combinations will leave you needing a cold shower!

Available now in ebook and print from Samhain Publishing.

What would you dare for a freefall of desire and passion?

Falling in Controlled Circumstances
© 2008 Pepper Espinoza

For four years, Gregory Jackson and his partner, Cambridge police chief Phillip Baker, have enjoyed a committed relationship. Neither suspect there's something missing in their lives. Until one fateful day when Phillip has a close call while on duty…and Gregory's flat tire puts him squarely in the glide path of dangerously charming American pilot Jim Tennant.

While Jim's in town to fly prototypes at the local air force base, Greg struggles to keep their relationship platonic, but Jim is an irresistible force. At the moment a transgression seems inevitable, Phillip surprises Gregory by encouraging him to take exactly what he wants. That night, all three of them really learn what it means to fly.

Gregory's pleasure is tempered by two serious concerns. Why is Jim interested in a relationship with a couple? And why is Phillip suddenly willing—even eager—to invite another man into their bed?

Warning: This title contains shameless flirting, playful banter, hot sex between two men, super-hot sex between three men, rule breaking and having fun.

Available now in ebook from Samhain Publishing.

GREAT
CHEAP
FUN

Discover eBooks!

THE FASTEST WAY TO GET THE HOTTEST NAMES

Get your favorite authors on your favorite reader, long before they're
out in print! Ebooks from Samhain go wherever you go, and work with
whatever you carry—Palm, PDF, Mobi, and more.

Samhain
Publishing Ltd

LaVergne, TN USA
25 February 2010
174314LV00001B/159/P